THE BOY
WHO
ESCAPED
PARADISE

ALSO BY J. M. LEE

THE INVESTIGATION

THE BOY

WHO

ESCAPED

PARADISE

J. M. LEE

TRANSLATED FROM THE KOREAN BY CHI-YOUNG KIM

PEGASUS BOOKS
NEW YORK LONDON

THE BOY WHO ESCAPED PARADISE

Pegasus Books Ltd
148 West 37th Street, 13th Floor
New York, NY 10018

Copyright © 2016 by J. M. Lee
Translated from the Korean by Chi-Young Kim

First Pegasus Books hardcover edition December 2016

Interior design by Sabrina Plomitallo-González, Pegasus Books

ISBN: 978-1-68177-252-3

10 9 8 7 6 5 4 3 2 '1

Printed in the United States of America
Distributed by W. W. Norton & Company, Inc.

THE BOY
WHO
ESCAPED
PARADISE

DAY ONE: PYONGYANG
FEBRUARY 1988–NOVEMBER 2000

NEW YORK DAILY NEWS

Man Found Shot to Death in Home in Queens
March 1, 2009

New York Police Department officials said Saturday that a man in his fifties was found shot to death in a Queens home. Officers arrived on the scene around 2 a.m. in response to a 911 call reporting several gunshots. The victim, Steve Yoon, defected from North Korea and was granted asylum two years ago. According to reports, he was the head of Friends of Freedom, a human rights organization.

Sources said that the victim's face had been wiped with antiseptic. Mysterious numbers and pictures were scrawled in blood around the body. Officials arrested an unidentified man at the scene. According to hospital sources, the suspect is in stable condition after being treated for a bullet wound to the thigh. Antiseptic and the victim's blood were detected on his hands, sources said.

Officials are focusing on the victim's past employment at major North Korean government facilities. Upon arriving in the U.S., Yoon provided information about the secluded country's nuclear program. A police official said, "We aren't sure if this is a straightforward murder or something more. We are considering every possibility, including an act of retribution by North Korea to punish the information leak."

★

1 11 21 1211 111221 312211.

ಬಬ

I'm a liar.

A m I a liar? I open my eyes. I'm in a square, windowless room, steel bars lining one side. I'm in bed. Pain shoots up my right thigh. I peer at it. It's wrapped in white bandages. A man is sitting next to me, talking at me. He tells me I was arrested at a murder scene. I was discovered unconscious. Apparently someone died and I killed him. Who was it? Did I kill someone? I can't remember. I don't know why I was there. Why would I kill him? Who killed him?

The death is a complicated equation that I am unable to solve. Two unknown variables and one constant—c_1 is death and c_2 is the murderer, and I am the constant. To solve for c_1 I must first find c_2, and to find c_2 I have to know c_3. All I know is that someone is dead and I'm supposed to be the murderer. $c_2 = c_3$. But what if I'm not c_2? What if I'm not c_3?

What do I know about c_1? Flicking a light switch—that's what death is like. Eyes that once twinkled remain closed; a heart that once beat sixty times a second is stilled. Nothing continues. Everything ends. 1 becomes 0.

The cell door opens and more men enter; one tall, the second short, the third with a crooked nose, the fourth muscular, and the last with a receding hairline. They look serious. They pitch questions at me. I think of Randy Johnson's fastballs.

"Name?"

"Age?"

"Birthplace?"

"Address?"

"Where were you on the night of February twenty-seventh?"

"Did you know the victim well?"

"Why did you kill him?"

"What happened that night?"

These aren't questions; it's chaos. I can't stand it. I start screaming. The man with the crooked nose clamps his hand over my mouth, his nose looming over me. His face is asymmetrical. His grip is unrelenting. It's a lobster claw. He hauls me off the bed and throws me on a chair. He announces that he is FBI agent Russell Banks. He calls me a murderer. A terrorist. Banks tells me they found the following on my body:

★ A blue dragon tattoo on my right forearm.

★ A bullet wound on my thigh.

★ Four scars on my torso, seven on my lower body, all of which are at least an inch long.

★ Evidence of my left pinky having been broken.

Then he tells me they found the following in my knapsack:

★ A 750 ml bottle of antiseptic and cotton balls.

★ Four fake passports—issued by China, Macau, South Korea, Japan.

★ Chinese, English, and Korean newspapers and magazine clippings.

★ Nineteen sheets filled with mathematical formulas and an unidentifiable language.

★ A small, worn notebook titled *The Possibilities of the Impossible*.

★ Two triangles, a three-meter-long tape measure, and an old Japanese-made calculator.

Banks grimaces. "All these fake passports! And all these aliases. Jiang Jiajie, Wei Zhenmin, Ahn Gil-mo, Matsumoto Yoji. Who are you, really? What's your relationship to all of these names?"

I am silent. It's not that I don't know the meaning of relationship: the way two or more concepts, objects, or people are connected, or the state of being connected. I know what it means to "have a relationship." I understand mathematical and scientific relationships, such as the relationship between Mercury and Venus or the black hole and the stars, as well as concepts like functional, symmetrical, and proportionate relationships. But the relationship between me and someone else? Or me and the world?

Banks's eyebrows furrow. "Explain yourself!"

He wants me to be frightened, but I'm not. Most people are scared of the incomprehensible or of uncertain fate. Not me. I think it's because relationships are challenging for me.

Banks grabs me by the front of my shirt and throws me on the floor. Hard fists and shiny shoes. I am a wet, crumpled tissue. He can break me apart, but my silence will stay intact. On the other side of the bars, the hallway dims. The chair, desk, and gray walls around me melt away. The agent's glowering face becomes fuzzy.

The door clangs open. "Stop!" cries a sharp female voice.

Banks's grip loosens. Blood shoots to my head. I drag my stiff leg to push myself up. "I'm in the middle of an interrogation," warns Banks. "This guy is on Interpol's most wanted list."

"This man is a patient," the woman argues. "You know it's against policy."

Banks shoves me into the chair and turns to glare at the intruder. "Look, all these passports are fake. He's linked to a dozen crimes, from fraudulent gambling to drug trafficking to murder. Whether he talks or not, he's going away for the rest of his life."

Now that blood is coursing throughout my body again, I can see. The woman is blond and is wearing white. She's a bit round and her cheeks are starting to sag; she stands confidently, like a rock, radiating authority. "Please consult with me before you interrogate him. I have to examine him right now, so step aside."

"Who are you, anyway?"

"Angela Stowe, nurse in charge," she snaps.

Banks and his men hesitate for a moment before leaving.

Angela takes my temperature: 97.7 Fahrenheit. 36.5 Celsius. She writes it down in her chart.

What kind of person is this Angela Stowe? I should create a puzzle to help me figure her out. The way someone approaches and solves a puzzle says a lot. An impatient person gives up quickly, while a cunning one guesses the answer and works backward. Of course, I like solving puzzles, myself. I feel a thrill when I extract simplicity from complexity. Everything falls into place when I organize chaos. I revel in that solitary moment when I encounter a problem, the time I wrestle with it, and the struggle against the urge to give up. All puzzles are equally fascinating, from problems composed of marbles to folding paper, dice, shapes, matches, ladybugs, knots, curves, and straight lines.

I write this down on a sheet of paper.

♋ ⅏ ♉

I think about my temperature: 36.5 Celsius. Three hundred sixty-five days in a year.

Angela picks up the sheet of paper. She places it on her chart and scribbles. She holds it out:

$$\top \Uparrow \text{\ss}$$

That's it! She thinks the way I do.

"Symmetry is the most beautiful characteristic in the world," Angela declares. "And the most beautiful number is a prime number." She gets me.

There's beauty in the puzzle I offered her, and she finds it beautiful, too. The heart is a symmetrical representation of the number 2, the first prime number. The clover is a mirror image of the next prime number, 3. The key is what you get when you flip the next prime number: 5. And her symbols pick up after my sequence.

She glances at me. "What I love about symmetry is that it never changes, no matter what you do. If you flip a heart, it's still a heart. If you flip a clover to the left or to the right, or up and down, it's still a clover. A circle is always a circle, and a sphere remains a sphere. I see that you like symmetry, too. So you believe in the truth, right? No matter what you do, the truth is always the truth."

Does she also like ABBA, my favorite band, with the symmetrical name? I feel a bit more comfortable. I think I can talk to her. "The equal sign is my favorite," I say, then pause. Should I go on? "No matter how long and complicated a formula is, the equal symbol makes both sides the same."

I begin drawing a triangle on the paper with = in the middle. My favorite shape.

$$1 \times 1 = 1$$
$$11 \times 11 = 121$$
$$111 \times 111 = 12321$$
$$1111 \times 1111 = 1234321$$
$$11111 \times 11111 = 123454321$$
$$111111 \times 111111 = 12345654321$$

Angela looks at me and then at my pyramid. "Where are you from?" Her question is different from Banks's, gentle and smooth.

I look down at my beautiful pyramid. "That doesn't matter. What's important is where we are and where we're going."

"I suppose that's true," Angela says, nodding. "It may not be important. It's just that the drawings you just did are identical to what they found at the scene of the murder. It's all over now. Why don't you tell me what happened? You can tell me whatever you remember."

I stare down at the sheet of paper. A giant pyramid rises through the fog of my memories. I see the city of weeping willows, the one I left long ago, and the pointy top of the high-rise I could see no matter where I was.

MY BIRTHDAY IS FEBRUARY 29

The Ryugyong Hotel stood tall in the Potong River District in west Pyongyang. Everyone referred to it as the 105 Building. Originally designed to be one hundred stories tall, it grew five more levels in honor of the 105th Shock Troops, which were in charge of the building's construction and directly under the purview of the Party Central Committee. The 435,000-square-meter hotel was to have had 3,700 rooms; it would boast seventy high-speed elevators, an underground swimming pool, five rotating observatory restaurants, a television station, and a meteorological station. From above, it formed a polygon of triangles and pentagons, and from the front it was a pyramid, its forty-story peaks clustered around the 105-story center.

I was born in 1988, the year after the 105 Building was born; neither of us was completed. The building was scheduled to be finished in April 1992, to commemorate the Great Leader's eightieth birthday, but the French joint engineering team left Pyongyang in May 1989, after the outer frame was constructed. The exterior was eventually finished but the interior stayed empty. Like me. I'm twenty-one, but people say I'm like a child. It's because my birthday is February 29. It takes Earth one year to circle the sun. Rather, it takes Earth 365.2564 days. That's 365 days, 6 hours, 15 minutes, and 23.04 seconds. So every four years, one day is left over, and that's my birthday. Since I age only one out of every four years, I suppose I'm about six years old now.

I like my birthday. Two and 29 are both prime numbers. Adding them up, you get 31, also a prime number. Prime numbers are solitary, like me. Even though it's not a prime number, four is also a good number. The Olympics, the World Cup, and the American presidency are on a four-year cycle. Four-year colleges and four-person tables are nice, and baseball is my favorite sport, since you have to go past first, second, and third bases to make it home, the fourth base, to score. Obviously my favorite batter is the clean-up hitter. I'm happy when the clock says 11:11—a perfect bilateral symmetry that adds up to four.

Our similarities made me interested in that enormous unfinished pyramid. I would look up at the empty building, calculating the radial angle of a triangle composed of the building's 160-meter-long base and its height. I calculated the area of the ground floor and how much the eighty-eighth floor shook when the wind was at thirty kilometers per hour. Sometimes I solved several questions quickly. Other times, one question would take me days to figure out. One such example was put into motion when Father opened his two-day-old copy of *Rodong Sinmun* one day. "Did you know that you can see Mount Taesong and the Nohak Mountain Range from the top of the Ryugyong Hotel?" he asked, reading an article to that effect. "On a clear day, you can even see the smoke rising from the Nampo smelter! That's one hundred *ri* away. How tall could that building be?"

His offhand comment piqued my interest. I ran over to the building the very next day. Rust bloomed on the outer concrete. Chunks of concrete had fallen off the steel beams. Soldiers stationed at the entrance ignored me. The sun glinted at the top of the building. Time inched along. As the sun set, the shadow of the tip grew wispy. I stood at the edge of the shadow as it inched across the plaza, revealing its secrets. The sun shined on the pyramid and me at the same angle as we both stood at ninety degrees to the ground. We were composed right-angle triangles. The ratio between my height and my shadow would be the same as the pyramid's.

$$a:b = x:c$$

If a was my height, b was the length of my shadow. Therefore, x was the pyramid's height, and c was the length of the pyramid's shadow.

Expressed as ratios, the formula was:

$$a / b = x / c$$

Then solve for x:

$$x = ac / b$$

Thus I could calculate the height of the pyramid by multiplying my height and the length of the pyramid's shadow and dividing it by the length of my shadow.

The next day, I went back to the hotel with a thirty-centimeter wooden ruler and a long string. I laid the string against the pyramid's shadow and then mine at 9 a.m., at 2 p.m., and right before sunset, and measured. It was a little tricky calculating the distance from the outer wall to the center of the building without stepping foot inside, but I figured I could determine the distance between the three wings that supported the building at a 120-degree angle by dividing it in half; the angle of each corner was 60 degrees. I used trigonometry to find the length of the hypotenuse, the diameter of the circle circumscribing the three wings, which was the distance between the outer wall and the center of the building.

The average height of the pyramid, taken in nine measurements over three days, was 323 meters. Three hundred twenty-three meters, compared to my 127 centimeters. The Potong River's warm wind embraced both of us as we stood under the same sun.

THE DELIVERER OF DEATH

I first saw the pale face of death at the Revolutionary Martyrs' Cemetery on Mount Taesong. The forest was dark, the sky was ash, the tombstones were even darker. Lips were firmly closed; the silence was white. The hole in the ground was dark. Mourners stood still, swallowing sobs. The black coffin was lowered into the hole. Wet dirt filled it up as voices tumbled along the ground. The ceremonious rifles hammered through it all. I imagined the dead floating up into the sky to become stars.

Father delivered death. He polished it and cared for it, mending crooked expressions, stitching wounds, and straightening postures. He wiped faces with antiseptic and painted lips red. Under Father's careful hands, the dead were reborn in elegance. When he was young, Father had been a talented surgeon at Pyongyang Medical University. One day, the highest-ranking officer in the Ministry of the People's Armed Forces was wheeled into the emergency room, covered in burns. There had been an explosion. The officer's death caused the revocation of Father's medical license; it was determined that Father's faltering loyalty to the Party had killed the man. But Father was let off easy; the authorities took into consideration the patient's critical condition. So he was demoted to undertaker at a hospital morgue located in an exclusive residential neighborhood in the Potong River District. The first death he delivered was that of the officer he'd failed to save. Party leaders and high-level military personnel began coming his way after meeting their demise, their family members seeking the talented former surgeon's services.

At the cemetery, I stared at the damp mound of dirt. "Where is death delivered?"

Father's jaw tensed. I recognized that expression. He looked that resigned when people called me an idiot, when he learned that I didn't have any friends, and when he realized that I didn't know how to play common childhood games, like soccer or war.

"I mean, when you die, your belongings go everywhere," I explained. "An old mattress will go to a colleague, teacups go to a married daughter, and a worn uniform goes to a son. Everything you leave behind is burned or thrown out or given away. So then where do the dead go?"

"Nobody really knows," Father said. "There's no use trying to understand it. I don't know myself, and I work with the dead every day."

But I was still curious. What happened inside funeral homes? What about in the cemeteries and the graves? What were the people in black thinking? I began to wander around the cemetery. I would get lost, then fall asleep on a grave. When he couldn't find me, Father learned to venture into the cemetery and carry me home on his back. "Not afraid of death, are you?" he'd murmur. "What a brave boy."

That wasn't quite it. I wanted to study death. I had to understand it. And to understand something, I had to figure out how it worked numerically. I was certain I could calculate the value of death without dying myself. After all, I had figured out the height of the 105 Building without going inside. But Father preferred that I focus on life.

The first time I was allowed to accompany him into the room where he washed and shrouded corpses, I strode in calmly. I took in the glistening metal gurney, the shiny wet wooden floor, the bright white incandescent lights, the sting of alcohol, the cool air, and the body lying neatly prone.

Father glanced at me nervously.

"Death is 0 and life is 1," I announced.

"Gil-mo, death isn't as simple as the binary system." Father straightened his white cap and stepped toward the body. "I help lead the dead to Paradise," Father said as he wiped the man's forehead with an antiseptic-soaked cotton ball.

"But we're already living in Paradise," I reminded him.

Father shook his head. "Paradise is where souls go to live. When people die, their souls survive. Just like a heart can die but the medals of revolutionary martyrs that hang over it stay constant. Or how a pair of eyes can die but their glasses remain." He always knew how to explain things so that I understood.

About a year later, I wandered into the work area in Father's absence. I picked up a cotton ball, soaked it in alcohol, and wiped down a corpse. Father showed up. Horrified, he slapped the back of my hand, making me drop the cotton ball on the floor. Eventually, Father gave up hitting the back of my hand to make me stop. I was decent at it, since I wasn't afraid.

Though his career as a doctor was cut short, Father still respected and loved the Great Leader and the Dear Leader. The Great Leader's blessings had allowed him to deliver the deaths of revolutionary martyrs, labor heroes, and merited actors. In fact, Father was part of a thirty-eight-person team of undertakers, doctors, chemists, and biologists that sealed the Great Leader in his glass coffin on July 8, 1994.

Hardships continued. The following summer, floods and drought battered the nation. On January 1, 1996, *Rodong Sinmun*'s New Year's editorial began with an exhortation: "In remembrance of the hardship and indomitable spirit of the anti-Japanese partisans who shared insufficient food together to struggle against the Japanese military, we must continue on with the spirit of the Arduous March, which was born in the dense forest of Mount Paektu." People went hungry and began to die. Hardship and death formed an equation: when hardship reached an extreme, deaths increased; as death mounted, hardships grew exponentially. Father delivered many deaths, then more and more. As the years passed, crowds thinned from the streets. Father listened to an old, static-filled radio, singing along to the revolutionary songs broadcast by the Propaganda and Agitation Department.

"I want to believe that our hardship will be overcome," Father sang. "I want to believe that our future is bright. Even though the day-to-day is difficult, we tighten our belts and follow the General."

Our rations diminished. I yearned for rice—white, gleaming rice. Hunger gnawed at us. Numbers became a tangled spool of thread in my head. When I managed to untangle them, I realized I was even hungrier. Official statistics had that 220,000 died from starvation from 1995 to 1998. But my own calculations revealed that the official statistics had to be multiplied by 9.8 or 11 to arrive at the true number. That meant that two to three million died during those years.

In the spring of 1999, I went to Pyongyang First Middle School to take a test, pursuant to a special action of the Party Central Committee that decreed the admission of students with superior mathematics skills. Father walked me there. The school was a 2,800-square-meter, ten-story building in Sinwon-dong in the Potong River District, with a music room, a gymnasium, a swimming pool, a library, and twenty labs holding thousands of pieces of scientific equipment.

A teacher placed a sheet of paper on a desk, patted my shoulder reassuringly, and motioned for my father to leave the room. The door closed behind Father. I wrestled with the numbers on the paper, losing track of time. Eventually, I looked up. The teacher's mouth was hanging open. "Young man, where did you learn all of this?"

I rubbed my eyes, suddenly tired.

Father was brought back in. "He's never learned anything in a formal environment," he explained. "Because of how he is, he wasn't able to attend primary school."

"Your son just solved a problem that is given to first-year math majors at Kim Chaek University of Technology," the teacher exclaimed. "He would have no problem with the fifth-grade curriculum! He'll be critical for the revolutionary task specially mandated by the Dear Leader."

"What kind of revolutionary task requires the participation of a child who's never been to school?" asked Father, looking stunned.

"The International Mathematical Olympiad," explained the teacher. "As the Great General is promoting math and sciences, we decided to enter. It's open only to students under twenty who are not in university, so that takes out scholars at Kim Il-sung University and Kim Chaek University of Technology. That's why this school will represent the republic. Your son is probably in the top one tenth of one percent of the country. If we teach him well, he will become a revolutionary pillar, raising our flag throughout the world."

Two weeks later we received an acceptance letter. The day before school started, Father brought home a paper-wrapped parcel. Inside was a new school uniform. He also had a large ration bag filled with rice. For the first time in two years, each member of our three-person family ate a bowl of rice that night.

The next morning, Father helped me with my uniform. "Pyongyang First Middle School is the alma mater of the Beloved and Respected Leader," he told me. "It's where talented youth from all across the country come to study. Dr. Kim Man-ho, the biology teacher, is a former professor at Pyongyang Medical University, and Ahn Chi-woo, the math teacher, holds a doctorate. They're university-level instructors. You know Dr. So Sang-guk, the head of the physics department at Kim Il-sung University? The one who launched Kwangmyongsong-1? The Dear Leader generously gave him a sixtieth birthday feast. You'll grow up to be a math genius like him. Just forget about all the death, all right?"

He tied a red Children's Union scarf around my neck and stood back, beaming at me with pride. "You know how much the Great Father loves us, right? You must work hard to be his honorable son." He reached over to embrace me but caught himself just in time. He had remembered that I couldn't stand being touched.

On my way to school, I took note of the date, the day of the week, the temperature, the direction of the wind, the time the sun rose, the signs on stores that were still closed, people's clothing, and license numbers. I spotted one that started with 216. February 16, the Dear Leader's birthday. $2 + 1 + 6 = 9$. This was a good sign.

The principal thought it would be best for me to build mathematical knowledge systematically through the general curriculum, so I wasn't placed in the class that was actively practicing for the Olympiad. It would be to our advantage for me to appear when I was older, as I was already three years younger than my classmates.

✪ ✪ ✪

Jae-ha was the only friend I made in school. He had been at Sinuiju First Middle School when he transferred here under the same special measure. His skinny, tanned physique marked him as a country boy. After classes, he raced to the rest area, to the go board on the table, where he had become a fixture. Nobody could beat him, neither the math teacher who had taught at Kim Hyong Jik University of Education nor the physics teacher who used to work at the Scientific Isotopic Research Institute. Jae-ha defended his position fiercely. In a mere three months, he had won a legendary 372 games out of 372.

One day, I went up to the board, composed of nineteen lines across and nineteen lines down. I wanted to arrange the black and white stones in a symmetrical pattern along the corners, so that they would mirror each other if I folded the board in half or quarters. "Nineteen times nineteen is three hundred sixty-one," I said, gesturing at the board. "Three hundred sixty-one meeting points."

Jae-ha shook his head. "It's not three hundred sixty-one. It's three hundred sixty plus one. The earth circles the sun in three hundred sixty degrees. The last one is the sun." He rolled a white stone between his fingers. "The four corners of the board are the four seasons—spring, summer, fall, winter. And the four intersections are the spring equinox, summer solstice, fall equinox, and winter solstice."

I grabbed a handful of stones and placed them in three piles on the board.

Jae-ha stared at them, then took twenty-five stones and put them down next to my pile. He had understood me. "If you subtract the first pile out of the second, it's 5 – 1 = 4. If you subtract the second pile from the third, it's 13 – 5 = 8, which is 4 × 2. If you subtract the third from the fourth it's 25 – 13 = 12 = 4 × 3. If you calculate it the same way, the fifth pile is 41. 41 – 25 = 16 = 4 × 4." He laid out ten stones on the board.

$$
\begin{array}{ccccc}
 & & o & & \\
 & & o & & \\
o & o & o & o & o \\
 & & o & & \\
 & & o & & \\
 & & o & & \\
\end{array}
$$

"Can you move only one to make it five across and five down?" he asked.

I was in my element. I picked up the stone at the very bottom and placed it gently on top of the middle stone. The shape with bilateral symmetry was now symmetrical on the top and bottom, too.

$$
\begin{matrix}
 & & \textit{0} & & \\
 & & \textit{0} & & \\
\textit{0} & \textit{0} & \text{\textcircled{P}}\textit{0} & \textit{0} & \\
 & & \textit{0} & & \\
 & & \textit{0} & &
\end{matrix}
$$

"I love symmetry," I announced. "Symmetry never changes."

"Symmetry exists between people, too," Jae-ha pointed out. "Friends are symmetrical. Because friendship doesn't ever change."

That was the day we became friends.

❂ ❂ ❂

The Arduous March continued, as did skipped meals, people who no longer smiled, and the growing number of shuttered stores. Everything was silent. We were hungrier the more we talked. To take my mind off food, I solved inequalities, geometry problems, numerical progressions, and equations, and sought solutions and proofs.

At school, I worked on problems, my pencil speeding across the paper. Jae-ha came up behind me. "What are you doing?"

"I'm mathematically proving the Battle of Pochonbo. Considering all the variables, like the gravity of the leaf, the buoyancy of the water, the Great Leader's weight, the height of the tide, and the speed with which the leaf becomes wet, I'm trying to figure out how many leaves he needed to cross the river."

Jae-ha looked around, then leaned in close. "Do you really believe that the Great Leader crossed the Yalu River on a single leaf and crushed the Japs?" he whispered. "The Battle of Pochonbo is a complete lie. The Great Leader's brigade of partisans crossed the river on a raft and attacked the police substation. That much is true, but it was after the Japanese police had already fled. So then they burned down the firehouse, the township office, and the post office. They ended up only killing Japanese civilians and children! A restaurant owner and the son of a policeman died in the chaos."

I ignored him. I was certain that things were either mathematically possible or impossible. Everything was provable, from the fact that we lived on a sphere to the fact that if we folded the space we were living on, we could move to another star in the universe. Crossing the Yalu on leaves wasn't impossible. I knew that. I just needed to prove it.

Our world was constructed of shiny go stones and numbers. We challenged each other to different problems, changing variables and sometimes destroying what we were working on. We would collapse into a fit of giggles. Jae-ha was especially excited for me to join the Olympiad preparation class. "When you get there, you have to try a Coca-Cola," he insisted. "And a McDonald's hamburger."

I didn't particularly want to, but told him I would.

We spent time in the shady school garden, where we watched a kingdom of ants. They cut up dead cicadas with their strong jaws, tossed the carcasses on their backs, and waddled across the garden in a long, shiny, black line. We peered down ant holes. When we felt that the universe within would suck us in, we fled across the playing field. We leaned on either side of a large oak tree, creating an isosceles. Summer vacation was upon us.

✪ ✪ ✪

Banks tosses an old, yellowed notebook onto the table, then picks it up to shove it under my eyes. "This was in your backpack.

It says 1968. That's long before you were born. Where did you get this?"

I don't speak. He grabs me by the throat and shoves me against the wall. My legs go limp. I can't breathe. Blood rushes to my head.

The door opens. Angela.

Banks drops me. Angela rushes over to peer into my eyes. Banks kicks the cell door open and leaves in a huff.

Angela helps me to the chair. She unwraps the bandages on my leg and cleans the wound. She applies a new bandage. "You need to tell them about this notebook."

"Why?"

"They won't stop until you do."

"I have to meet Mr. Knight Miecher."

"Who's that?"

"I don't know," I answer truthfully. "But I have to return the notebook to him."

"How will you do that, when you don't even know who that is?"

"I just have to figure out the probability of meeting him. There are six billion people in the world. Two point two million people are in the republic, and there are 280 million Americans. So what are the odds that one citizen of the republic meets one American?"

"But that would be less than one out of several million, or even tens of million," Angela points out. "Maybe even less. Chances are you won't ever meet him."

"Even with those odds, something that needs to happen is bound to happen. No matter how rare it may be. Even the least possible thing isn't necessarily *im*possible."

Angela shakes her head. "Probability is relative, depending on the time and place and person," she says.

"I believe in the numbers."

Angela looks annoyed. "Numbers aren't everything." She picks up the notebook and flips through it. "How did you end up with this?"

I close my eyes. I'm back in Pyongyang. It's 1999. Sunlight shatters on the pavement. The Taedong River is teeming with gray mullet, their scales flashing. I see the dark cabin of the USS *Pueblo*, moored to the riverbank.

THE POSSIBILITIES OF THE IMPOSSIBLE

Jae-ha and I walked down the light-dappled streets of east Pyongyang. Leaves had fallen with the rain and the breeze rolled them along on the ground, their pale underbelly flashing the sky. The streetcar ran along the damp road, sounding its horn. Cars smelled of metal and gasoline. We were on our way to confirm a legend.

"It's a huge ship, bigger than a whale," Jae-ha said. "It's in the Taedong River. Senior Colonel Park In-ho is still guarding it. That's the soldier who captured it thirty-one years ago!"

He turned silent as we crossed Okryu Bridge and then Taedong Bridge. Gray apartment blocks loomed over us as we passed Pyongyang Grand Theater. Emaciated dogs scampered along the riverbank, their tongues lolling. A young man, sweating through his white shirt, walked under green Chinese juniper trees with a woman. We passed by Chungsong Bridge, erected where the *General Sherman*, the American steamer, sank under siege by Pyongyang residents in 1866.

An enormous steel mass appeared.

Jae-ha perked up. "The USS *Pueblo* has a displacement of nine hundred six tons. Fifty-four meters long, ten meters wide, and armed with machine guns! She can travel up to twelve knots."

The gray ship was menacing. I was sure it could swallow us whole. My heart hammered at 125 beats per minute. The ship's steel body had corroded somewhat, and the two tall transmission towers were bent. We used the stairs toward the stern to hop on board. An old man in a tall cap and white dress uniform was standing on the top deck near the machine gun. He looked like a tin soldier, a small, worn, useless part of the large ship. Colorful medals glinted on his chest.

Jae-ha strode up to him. "Are you Senior Colonel Park In-ho, the hero who captured the USS *Pueblo*?"

The old man nodded, looking at us curiously.

"We're students at Pyongyang First Middle School," explained Jae-ha. "We came to hear your story."

The senior colonel straightened, though his shoulders remained stooped. He balled his thin hands. "It was off the coast of Wonsan on January 23, 1968," he began. "I was a soldier on a Navy SO-1 patrol ship. Just after noon, an unidentified vessel appeared. It was a converted cargo ship, the USS *Pueblo*. An American National Security Agency spy ship loaded with cutting-edge wiretapping devices." The old man's waxy face flushed as he spoke about how he aimed the artillery at the vessel, demanding over the radio that they identify themselves; how the American flag was raised; how four torpedo boats arrived from Wonsan; how the Yanks claimed to be conducting a hydrograph-ical survey before fleeing to open waters; and how he was one of seven do-or-die squad members who leaped on a torpedo boat to chase them down. When they caught up to the USS *Pueblo*, they boarded her and captured eighty-two out of eighty-three men (one was killed in the skirmish), then steered the ship back to the harbor. He was sprightly now, his voice strong and clear. "We made these artillery marks," he said proudly, shoving his finger into a dark hole in the body of the ship.

He tried to pat my head, but I ducked away. He led us down a narrow hallway and brought us into a cabin converted into a display area. American navy uniforms, personal effects, and hats were on display. Yellowed documents in English were displayed in a glass case, including an apology from the American government declaring that it would cease spying activities, evidentiary documents about USS *Pueblo*'s surveillance activities, confessions and apologies by the spies, and an open letter sent to the American president. The mess hall was now a multimedia theater, where black-and-white footage was shown on a loop.

Every day, we walked along the Taedong River, following the gray mullets swimming with the current. Unlike the Potong River, which slapped and swished against the banks, the Taedong was silent; it came from 450.3 kilometers away, carving bluffs and gorges on its way to Pyongyang, carrying anthracite, zinc, and brown alluvial soil, and teeming with different species of trout, gray mullet, carp, catfish, and cornet fish. When we approached the USS *Pueblo*, the senior colonel would wave out a small paint-flecked glass window.

"The Yanks insisted on a ridiculous version of the story," the colonel huffed one day. "They said they were working in open waters when our patrol ships blasted them with fifty-seven millimeter machine guns. They called it an illegal military provocation! They screamed about retaliation. You see, it was the first time in their history that another country seized their warship. So they dispatched the USS *Enterprise* and several hundred bombers and fighter jets. But we weren't cowed at all. No, sir! While they threatened us publicly, they were engaging in twenty-eight behind-the-scenes negotiations with us. Finally, on December 23, 1968, they released a statement apologizing for their violation of our territorial waters. We returned eighty-two men and the one body but kept the ship and their equipment. They begged us to return the ship. It's been thirty years now, but we've been resolute."

Every time we went to the ship, I studied the English apology and the Korean translation. The words and sentences in the two languages organized themselves in my head, and new words embedded in my mind. One day, near the end of summer vacation, the senior colonel showed us the communications room. I spotted a complicated piece of equipment with numerous buttons and switches. I opened the equipment panel and saw smooth, shiny diode parts. I flipped through the English signal corpsman's manual and started to read the fundamentals of radio frequency out loud, hesitantly.

The senior colonel blinked his sleep-crusted eyes, amused. "If the Yanks heard your English, they would say you are very polite and formal, since you're learning it through apologies and manuals." He took us to the end of the narrow hallway. The cabin was laden with all kinds of gear—hats, boots, galoshes, compasses, lighters, and fountain pens, all piled on shelves. The senior colonel rummaged around and showed me an old, crinkly, water-logged notebook.

The Possibilities of the Impossible
—Odysseus, returning to Ithaca

Seawater had eroded the words inside. Careful script floated among blue ink spots. *When I return to you*, read a fragment, and another sentence stated *abeth, tonight, too, I will see you in my dreams.* I found another fragment: *your dress on our wedding day.*

"They're letters from a man called Odysseus to a woman named Abeth," I announced.

"His name wasn't Odysseus," the senior colonel corrected me. "His name was Captain Knight Miecher. He was the signal officer of the USS *Pueblo*."

"He left his notebook behind," I murmured.

"He wanted it back, but I couldn't give it to him. Not to an enemy fighter." The senior colonel sounded wistful.

"But you wanted to?" asked Jae-ha.

The colonel's eyes darted around. He rubbed his wrinkled mouth. "Strictly speaking, we were enemies, you know. When I volunteered on the do-or-die squad, we had the following mission. We had to get on the boat quickly and subdue them, then take away their weapons, cut communications, then bring the boat back to Wonsan. We pursued them on a torpedo boat and battered them with bullets. The men were running around, panicked, and that's when we jumped aboard."

"And they surrendered, just like that?" Jae-ha leaned forward. The senior colonel hadn't gone into the details before. "Or did they attack?"

"They were destroying electronics with axes and hammers. And burning classified documents. Anything they didn't have time to get to, they threw overboard. I ran up to the bridge, kicked open the door, and aimed my machine gun. I was going to let them have it. Inside were four men, who pointed their pistols at me. They were yelling something at me. I looked behind me, and that's when realized I was alone. My comrades had gone below deck, where most of the enemy soldiers were. I could shoot, but I knew I wouldn't be able to get all of them before they shot me dead. I thought of my wife. I thought I was a dead man."

Jae-ha's eyes grew wider in excitement.

"We were screaming at one another, unable to understand what the other was saying," continued the senior colonel. "It was tense. We were about to start shooting. But then an officer said something to the others. They yelled back at him. He reached out and took one man's gun, and the rest of them laid down their weapons. I didn't know what to do. That's when our support troops made it onboard and took over. One American sergeant died under fire and thirteen were wounded. I received the highest accolade for my role in the capture. But if it hadn't been for that officer, I would have ended up a corpse."

"And then what happened?" Jae-ha asked breathlessly.

"We brought the USS *Pueblo* into Wonsan. I still had my gun on the captain. I was drained, but still tense. The sun was beginning to set. We couldn't communicate, of course, but he told me his name was Knight Miecher. I paused, then said, 'I'm Park In-ho.' He offered me a drag on his cigarette. He took out his wallet and showed me a photo of himself with a smiling blonde, holding a young boy. His wife, you see. I showed him a picture of my wife, too."

The senior colonel paused for a moment. "In Wonsan," he said quietly, "we searched the men and confiscated their belongings. I took Captain Miecher's watch, ring, and dog tags. This notebook had gotten wet from the skirmish. He looked at me pleadingly but there was no way I could let him keep it. All the confiscated items were kept right on this ship. By the time I got my hands on the notebook, he had already been taken to Pyongyang with the other captives."

"Did you ever see Captain Miecher again?" Jae-ha asked.

The senior colonel lifted his cap off as he shook his head. A warm breeze floated upstream and puffed his white hair. He smoothed his white cotton ball of hair before replacing his hat on his head. "He went home eleven months later. It never sat right with me, you understand? Like I was interfering with his marriage. Or maybe stealing a piece of it away."

"You should return it to him," I interjected. "He should have this back."

"I told you, he went home decades ago. I'm never going to see him again. We were around the same age. There isn't much time left. Assuming he's still alive, he must be well over sixty."

"I'm still young," I said. "I can get it back to him."

The senior colonel looked down at his wrinkled hands. "That's true," he murmured. "Maybe you can."

The sun was setting on our way home. Darkness mingled with the scent of cut grass along the riverbank. The sun dipped in the river, turning it red, before sinking slowly. Gray mullet leaped out of the water, flashing their silver bellies, their backs speckled with open wounds from underwater fights with thin, slippery fins. We ran by Chungsong Bridge, Pyongyang Grand Theater, the Youth Alliance building. The streetcar squeaked atop the silver rails, passing emaciated dogs and dazed-looking people. We hurtled along. Jae-ha's tanned calves glowed ahead of me.

"Do you think Captain Miecher's still alive?" I asked, panting.

"I don't know. But even if he is, it's impossible to meet someone who lives in America."

Waist-high grasses brushed against our legs as we ran.

"Just because it's extremely unlikely doesn't mean it's impossible," I reasoned. "Coincidences and miracles happen all the time. If Captain Miecher is alive, he would be meeting someone right now. His wife or children or his soldiers, if he's still in the military. Meeting someone is ordinary for him, right? But if that someone is us, that's when it becomes a miracle. You can break down the probability of an occurrence as either the probability of something happening to someone or the probability of something happening to me. There's a lottery winner each week, but it would be a miracle for me to win."

"But not everyone can win the lottery," Jae-ha argued.

"It's more likely than you think," I explained. "Because we can be connected to anyone in the world in just six steps. You can be linked to Jiang Zemin or even Fidel Castro."

"What? That makes no sense," muttered Jae-ha.

"Sure it does. It's simple math. Look. Let's say you know one thousand people. If each of them knows another thousand people, it's 1,000 × 1,000 = 1,000,000. Of course, you have to suppose that everyone you're talking about knows different people, but in that way you can get to know a million people by going through one person. In just a few steps, we can be friends with everyone in the whole world." I had learned about this theory in a science magazine I found on the USS *Pueblo*. It included a profile of a Harvard psychology professor named Stanley Milgram. In 1967, he sent 160 Omahans a letter for a stockbroker in Boston, asking them to send it to someone they knew would be able to deliver the letter to the stockbroker. Forty-two letters were delivered to the correct destination, after going through an average of 5.5 people. Though everyone was scattered, people were linked together. That meant that a Chinese drug lord was linked to a Wall Street banker, and a Taliban soldier was linked to the person collecting tickets at Disneyland. That also meant that I had to be linked to Captain Miecher somehow. I would return his notebook to him.

With my first exposure to English on the USS *Pueblo* as the catalyst, I grew interested in studying the language in earnest. I memorized an entire English textbook. I went on to read books in English, then branched out into French, Russian, and Japanese, though I didn't necessarily understand what I was reading. Languages interested me, with their specific symbols and limited phonetic symbols that operated in a regular grammatical system. I lost myself in the study of phonetic symbols, rules, and sentence patterns. Even irregular verbs or idioms and their unconventional uses were linked to a loose framework of rules; these complications, I found, were beautiful. In the library, I read about superstring theory and the theory of complexity, the Riemann hypothesis, Gödel, and Gauss, all in English. My world expanded as I discovered the *Annals of Mathematics*, the

Journal of the American Mathematical Society, and *Physical Review Letters*, published by the American Physical Society.

I was partial to the single copy of *Newsweek*, that thin, shiny magazine beckoning with color photographs of the outside world. I read about Afghanistan, Al Qaeda, the rebirth of terrorism, the snare of globalization, IMF relief loans to South Korea, Steve Jobs, and Wall Street. Jae-ha's theory was that *Newsweek* was placed in the library so we would learn about the IMF bailouts to South Korea and America's struggles in Afghanistan. I just wanted to wear jeans and drink Coca-Cola. The word "dollar" reeked of abundance. That was what a capitalist must feel like, I thought, as I murmured the word under my breath.

THE CREATION OF BEAUTY

On January 1, 2000, Father read the New Year's editorial of the *Rodong Sinmun* out loud, his voice trembling with emotion. "Thanks to the people's struggle, the Arduous March that continued for many years has finally entered a march on the double." The four-year-long march—the march of death, hunger, poverty, and blood—was officially over. We survived, but Father had aged dramatically. That year, I entered the fourth grade.

One afternoon near the end of spring, I sat in the quiet rest area at school, studying the go board and its nineteen vertical and horizontal lines. A warm breeze danced gently in through the open window. I could see the flag flapping outside. Jae-ha walked in and perched on a tall round stool next to me. He spun counterclockwise. "It's almost summer."

He spun once, twice, three times. When he twirled, his face split in half, his teeth glistening white like fruit seeds. Six, seven . . . I thought of the senior colonel, his white hair and his tanned, lined face, his pressed uniform, colorful insignias, and gold epaulets. Nine, ten . . . "Do you think the senior colonel's still there?" I asked.

"Even if he is, we won't have time to go to the USS *Pueblo* this summer," Jae-ha reminded me. "Did you forget? Everyone in the fourth, fifth, and sixth grades has to practice for the mass games." Twenty-two, twenty-three . . . Jae-ha stopped spinning. He cocked his head and swallowed, looking green. "I hope it doesn't kill us." He hopped down, swaying.

The seat of the stool continued to spin. I waited until it halted and placed my palm on it, measuring it. It was the length of my palm and two joints on my pointer. "My palm is precisely fifteen centimeters and the end of my index finger is two centimeters. So the radius of the seat is $15 + 2 + 2 = 19$ centimeters. The circumference is $19 \times 2 \times 3.14 = 119.32$. So when the stool spins once it moves 119.32 centimeters."

"So?"

"The stool spun twenty-three times. So you moved 27.4436 meters while sitting still."

✪ ✪ ✪

That year was the fifty-fifth anniversary of the founding of the Workers Party, and the mass games would incorporate more than 100,000 participants, ten times more than the usual. The festival would showcase the glory of the nation's youth to the entire citizenry. Tens of thousands of students from Kim Il-sung University and Kim Chaek University of Technology were to practice under the glaring sun over six months in the Rungnado May Day Stadium, as would students in the upper three grades at our school.

My math teacher recommended me for the design committee, which was in charge of arranging hundreds of colored rectangles in the correct place, enabling the scenery to change during the performance. Midnight blue and white would become waves lapping the ridge of Mount Paektu, waves gathering and spreading out, lightning cutting across the scenery and a rainbow unfolding overhead. "A good grasp of geometry is required to create these scenes," explained my math teacher.

"This special performance will show everyone the creativity and math skills of our youth. It won't be easy. You'll have to create more than thirty original scenes and lay out when and in what order twenty thousand performers will hold up which cards."

After design, the images were assigned to specific schools, and each individual student was given a part. The students then pasted colored paper on cardboard to create hundreds of colored squares to be bound into a large book. On the back of each page were detailed instructions on the various movements; some required raising the card up, while others had them moving the card from side to side or waving it. My school was to be the middle of the scene, composing the Dear Leader and the Great General's faces. Jae-ha spent a full three days making his cardboard book. He had told me earlier that he wanted to be the Dear Leader's eyeball, so I placed him in the center of the Dear Leader's eye. He would be silver, the twinkle in his eye, surrounded by twenty thousand others forming the Dear Leader's noble face. I mapped out the Dear Leader's expressions in my notebook.

One late afternoon, Jae-ha came up behind me as I scribbled in my notebook. "What are you calculating this time?"

"The orbit of Kwangmyongsong-1, which will be launched into space from Rungnado May Day Stadium on the day of the performance. When you drop an object here on Earth, it gains speed every second it falls. The satellite can use the power from that and circle Earth forever. So the energy needed for a satellite that enters orbit is zero." I was about to expand on the structure and flight principle of the satellite, propulsion device, and orbit design, but stopped short when Jae-ha laughed.

"We're not launching a real satellite, Gil-mo," he said kindly. "It's the mass games. Kwangmyongsong-1 is part of the scenery. You can't really send it into orbit."

I ignored him. I would finish my calculations and launch my satellite at the stadium, watching as it entered the quiet orbit of space and began its endless, oval journey.

Practice began before dawn and continued late into the night. Students fainted under the hot sun and gymnasts ruptured ligaments. But practice continued. Once each school mastered its part, the entire group of 100,000 assembled at the Rungnado Stadium every day for three months. Students sat in seats marked with coordinates and opened and closed 150 different cards to enact an enormous scene. Below the premier's seat, the head conductor from the Physical Education Guidance Committee oversaw the actions of each school with flag signals. In order to open and close the cardboards in perfect unison, one had to memorize all the cardboard numbers and their sequence to revolutionary songs. When done correctly, the background became a huge screen.

Jae-ha picked me up at dawn every morning, his bag weighed down by his colorful cardboards. At noon, we got a short lunch break, though only three or four out of ten could afford to bring lunch. Some filled their stomachs with water, but as we weren't allowed to go to the bathroom during practice, they ended up pissing in their seats. Hunger and full bladders turned lips white, which flaked like salt. The sun burned faces raw before turning them dark. Through it all, the music blared on, students opened colorful cardboards, and the choreography continued. One board signified nothing, but twenty thousand boards moving together created something beautiful. And I had designed it. As the performance date drew near, the students grew withdrawn, hungry, and exhausted. Nobody laughed or talked anymore. Three days before the performance, we were all given a special distribution of extra corn and flour.

On the morning of the performance, before the sun was

even up, the Rungnado Stadium was boisterous from students assembling by school and by grade. Laser lights, an enormous projector and a slide projector, and sound equipment were installed throughout the stadium. The director's voice boomed from the speakers. "Tonight, this important performance will determine the republic's fate. The Dear Leader will watch the performance with a special delegation, headed by U.S. Secretary of State Madeleine Albright, which has come to apologize for the evil aimed at the republic and to normalize relations. With this performance by the ever victorious Workers Party, we will show that we stand united behind the military power of the republic and the Dear Leader."

Later, we were given two hours for lunch to allow sufficient rest. Jae-ha came down from the scenery section, settled at the bottom of the stairs, and shoveled boiled corn in his mouth.

"So if we perform for the Yankees," I asked Jae-ha, "does that mean we're now friends?"

Jae-ha's mouth was full of salted radish. "I don't know, but I wish they could come every day if it means we could get a special distribution each time."

At three p.m., citizens of Pyongyang poured into the stadium. Women were dressed up in beautiful *hanbok*, some in jade and others in purple. Men wore Mao suits or military uniforms. The setting sun dyed the stands as darkness crept across the stadium. Spotlights popped on. The audience roared. To grand music, the sun rose above Mount Paektu in the scenery. The words *Eternal Sun* appeared, and the spotlight shined on the dais in the VIP viewing area.

"The Dear Leader and U.S. Secretary of State Albright have entered the viewing area and are now seated," intoned the voice overhead.

The head conductor raised his flag. The word *Welcome!*

appeared against a yellow background, in both English and Korean. Applause and shouts rang out. I looked out as music throbbed through the stadium. A yellow sunflower bloomed and turned into a large circle. I calculated the number of petals—eight—and the diameter of the resulting circle—1.25 times greater than the original flower.

At that very moment, my rocket began to shoot sparks and let out a huge boom. The republic's flag was clearly visible on its side as it shook and shot out plumes of smoke. The audience thundered, raising their hands in the air.

The principle of the rocket could be explained through the Tsiolkovsky rocket equation. $\Delta v = v \ln(m0/m1) + v0$. Δv was the maximum change of velocity of the rocket. $m0$ was the rocket's mass, $m1$ was the rocket's mass without propellant, $v0$ was the rocket's initial speed, and v was the propellant's jet velocity. Δv became larger the bigger v and $m0$ were and the smaller $m1$ was.

With a large boom, the rocket shot up out of the scenery into the air, leaving behind sparks. The stadium roared. The rocket grew smaller in the darkness before flickering and disappearing.

According to my calculations, the satellite on the rocket would reach orbit 280 kilometers above ground in twenty-eight minutes and begin to circle the earth.

A flock of white doves flew up in the scenery. My design allowed for 284 doves. At first, 64 flew up, then 220 followed them. 284 and 220 were amicable numbers. 220's factor is 1, 2, 4, 5, 10, 11, 20, 22, 44, 55, 110, and 284's factor is 1, 2, 4, 71, 142. The sum of 220's factor is 284, and the sum of 284's factor is 220. Math is beautiful, the way the world is.

The next morning, Father was holding the *Rodong Sinmun* when I woke. He read a particular article out loud to me.

On Historic Visit to the Republic
U.S. Secretary of State Madeleine Albright Changes
American Flag Pin to Heart Brooch
October 24, 2000

U.S. Secretary of State Madeleine Albright arrived at Sunan Airport on October 23. After paying respects at the Kumsusan Memorial Palace, where the Great Leader is laid to rest, she entered three hours of talks with the Dear Leader at the Paekhwawon Guesthouse, where she is staying. Afterward, Secretary Albright viewed the performance by the ever-victorious Workers Party at the Rungnado May Day Stadium. At the banquet hall, she appeared without the American flag pin she had been wearing in her initial meetings with the Dear Leader, instead donning a heart-shaped brooch.

Secretary Albright, known for her "brooch diplomacy," wears pins depicting bees, eagles, and scorpions when dealing with hostile countries, and butterflies when meeting with allies. When the Middle East discussions were stalled, she wore a bicycle brooch, urging continuous advancement. The American flag pin likely signaled her firm position at the talks, while the heart pin suggests her hopes for friendly relations between the countries. However, the precise reason for the sudden change in adornment remains unclear.

The cell door screams as it closes. Banks looks at me with hostility. "1, 11, 21, 1211, 111221, 312211. What do these numbers mean? You wrote them in blood next to the body."

I don't answer. He keeps asking questions, glaring at me. I tune him out and think about beautiful things. Numbers and figures, theorems and hypotheses, proofs and solutions, symmetrical expressions. 47 and 74. 47 plus 74 is 121. 39 and 93 reveals an even more profound symmetry. If you add the two, you get 132, which isn't itself symmetrical but if you flip it, you get 231, and if you add that to 132, you get 363. I look up to see Angela standing behind Banks.

"The numbers themselves, they don't mean anything," she tells him.

Banks glances back at her. "It was written in the victim's blood. At the scene of the crime. It could mean something."

Angela shoots me an imperceptible smile. "It's just a sequence of numbers. The first is one. One one. You write that out, and you get eleven. That's two ones, right? So then the next is twenty-one, which is one two and one one, so that makes it 1211. That's one one, one two, and two ones, so the next is 111221. And so forth. It just shows that someone with Asperger's was panicking. In a state of half-suspended animation, the person fled into the world of numbers."

"Asperger's? This kid has Asperger's?"

"You clearly don't understand the whole picture, although

you know quite a lot about this young man," answers Angela without bothering to look up from her file. "You can't make him talk. Threats don't work on him, and your questions don't, either."

"How would you know?" Banks snaps.

"People with Asperger's have difficulties in social situations but they don't have an issue with language. He's not going to respond to standard interrogation tactics. Do you see? Stop bullying the patient, please. You can go now. I have to examine him."

Banks gives up and leaves the room.

I write down a symmetrical expression. I = A. I is me, A is Angela. We both love numbers, particularly prime numbers, and we appreciate symmetry. I can tell we both see beauty in the world.

"Did you kill him?" asks Angela gently. "And did you really commit all those other crimes?"

"No."

"But you were found at the scene. And you're wanted by Interpol."

"I don't know what to do," I mumble.

"Why don't you tell me the rest of your story?" she suggests. "Maybe I'll be able to help you."

I hesitate. Should I? Wasn't it Aristotle who said that you have to reach the fundamentals of something if you want to understand it?

She takes my temperature and squints at the thermometer. "You have more than ten stab wounds," she continues casually. "Your bones were broken."

"I can prove why a digon doesn't exist," I tell her.

Angela rips out a piece of paper from my medical chart. She

hands me a pen. I enter the quiet world of numbers. She studies my work. "Where did you learn this?"

"I learned everything from the streets."

"How so?"

I tell her it's a long story. It all happened a long time ago.

THREE FATHERS

SPSD agents burst into our apartment on November 29. They overturned the table, ripped up the floorboards in the bathroom, and threw dishes on the ground. The household's symmetry collapsed, tipping the balance. I carefully put things back in their place as the agents ripped off wallpaper, rummaged through the closet, and punched holes in the ceiling. They finally found it—a blue book buried deep in the closet. Father's eyes clouded over. The SPSD officers bent my parents' arms behind their backs and took them away. They were barely given enough time to put their shoes on. I was left alone in the mess.

The next day, my math teacher arranged to have me stay at the school dormitory. Jae-ha gave me his bed and took the floor.

"Why did they take my parents away?" I asked into the darkness.

"Because of that book, no?" murmured Jae-ha.

When day broke, other students began to glare at me. Whispers floated from person to person—traitor, political offender, Jesus lover, prison. They cut my skin as they flew past.

"Don't worry," my math teacher said. "Your parents are probably fine." His face was grim, though, and his eyes were troubled. Something was happening, but I didn't know what.

On Sunday afternoon, Jae-ha and I headed to the USS *Pueblo* for the first time in a while. The banks of green grass had yellowed, and the river was quiet. The barren weeping willow branches swept against one another. Fish no longer leaped out of the water. Everything seemed changed.

The senior colonel poked his head out from the top of the bridge. He was grizzled and perhaps a bit more frail. There were no other visitors. We followed him to the bottom of the ship. He wheezed when he talked and let out a dry cough whenever he paused. Jae-ha told him that my parents were taken by the SPSD. The senior colonel's expression darkened. He led us into the gallery and equipment lock. I took comfort in my routine, reading the confession and joint announcement and studying the communications equipment. The senior colonel went into the cabin and brought something for me. "Take it," he urged. "It's Knight Miecher's notebook."

"I'd like to meet Captain Miecher," I said. "I'll get this back to him."

The senior colonel nodded. "You did say people are linked together. You can meet anyone in the world through six steps, right? Please get it back to him. But don't tell anyone about it."

"Why not?"

"Because if you talk about it, people will think you're crazy."

✪ ✪ ✪

We returned to the dormitory to find our math teacher in his coat, waiting for me. "Gil-mo, you can go home now. I'll take you."

Jae-ha trailed after us.

The apartment didn't seem like ours. We had enjoyed precarious comfort and a delicate peace, but now, it felt unsettled and nerve-wracking. Father was sitting in the living room, defeated and somber. His face was no longer symmetrical, with one eye the color of a plum and a lump swelling on his forehead. He avoided my gaze. "Pack your knapsack. Take only necessities."

Where was Mother? What did I need? What should I leave behind? I began to gather my belongings. Two pairs of long underwear. Winter pants.

"Take your summer uniform," Father called.

We weren't going to be home next summer? Were we ever coming back? I packed my toothbrush, a cup, a pair of worn shoes, a winter hat with earflaps, spare buttons in a round tin, two wooden dice, a compass and protractor, a thirty-centimeter ruler, and a three-meter-long tape measure.

"Just the necessities!" snapped Father. "What do you need all of that for?" He stood up, his joints cracking. On the other side of our torn curtains, four SPSD agents were waiting behind a military truck parked in the dark. Their breaths were white against the night. Father swung a heavy black bag over his shoulder.

"What about Mother?" I asked.

"She won't be coming with us."

Where was she?

My math teacher took his glasses off and used his sleeve to polish them. "Gil-mo, the world is a beautiful place. Don't forget that, all right?"

"It's beautiful because it's made of numbers," I reminded him.

He nodded, then slid his hand in his inner pocket. He hesitated before taking out an old calculator. "When things get difficult, look at the numbers that appear on the screen. You'll remember that the world is a beautiful place." He put it in my knapsack.

Jae-ha pulled his gloves off and helped me put them on. The agents yanked my knapsack away and tossed it on the cargo bed of the truck. They pushed me and Father on. The truck began to rattle down the alley. Jae-ha began running after the truck. He held out a hand. I grabbed it. The truck sped up, and his hand was pulled out of my grasp. He tumbled to the ground. "Gil-mo!" he called, his voice cracking. "Take care, Gil-mo!" And then the only friend I had was out of sight. Jae-ha, whose sleeves didn't cover his wrists because he grew so quickly, whose upper lip was dark with the beginnings of a moustache, whose mastery of go was astounding.

"At least you don't understand what's going on," Father murmured next to me.

He was wrong, though. I understood everything.

Father had lied to Mother and me. He had secretly become Christian, believing in the father in heaven. Everyone in the republic had two fathers: the one who returned home every night, reeking of sweat, only to gaze at his hungry family's vacant eyes, and the Great Father, who looked over his sons and daughters from the portrait hanging in every home, from the enormous statue on Changgwang Street, from the advertising tower, from everywhere, really, in the nation. But neither man could sate their children's hunger. My father, I suppose, had needed a new father. He had managed to get his hands on a popular-edition Bible, smuggled in from China and circulated in secret. My ideology teacher told us that fear made people look to God, and reminded us that we must be warriors for the republic and not give in to fear. But everyone was afraid. We all celebrated the Great Father and the Dear Leader because of our fear. Father was afraid, too, and faith revealed itself to him one day, the day he delivered the death of a young factory worker.

The dead man's mother, instead of wailing and fainting, closed her eyes quietly, her face suffused with peace, her lips moving imperceptibly. After the funeral, my father went up to her. "I hope you won't mind my asking this," he said. "Mothers who lose their sons are grief-stricken. How are you able to remain so calm?"

She looked at him carefully. "It's because I believe he went to a peaceful place."

Father was intrigued. Two months later, the dead man's mother handed him a small blue book, and he became a member of an underground church. Without telling anyone, he embraced another father. Even as he secretly prayed to his father in heaven, he remained loyal to the Great Father and the Dear Leader. Over bowls of watery corn gruel, he reminded us that we should be grateful to the Great Father. Mother would ladle milky broth into my bowl and glare at him. "This corn gruel isn't going to fill us," she snapped. "What should we be grateful for?"

"For everything," Father would reply serenely.

I would slurp up the broth and look longingly at Father's bowl, and he would, without fail, push his bowl toward me, although two servings of corn gruel inevitably gave me diarrhea all night. Once, I woke in the middle of the night for yet another trip to the bathroom. On my way back to bed, I spotted Father kneeling in the dark living room, murmuring quietly. I watched him quietly. A long time later, he stopped talking to himself and glanced at me. "I'm praying for the death I delivered today."

"Do they come back to life if you do?"

"No, a prayer is a stamp you put on the dead. It helps their souls reach heaven safely."

Did the dead want to go there? Back in bed, I wondered what happened if the souls wanted to come back. What happened if the dead were delivered to the wrong place?

In the end, instead of sating our hunger, Father's god had sent us to prison camp.

⟡ ⟡ ⟡

The truck hurtled through the darkness. Cold air stung my face. Father hunched toward me in an attempt to shield me from the wind, but he was too thin to block much of anything. He took his scarf off and wound it around my neck.

"How could you fool us all like that?" I asked him.

Father spoke haltingly. "I decided to think of the Great Father as the father in heaven and his son, the Dear Leader, as Jesus Christ. So when I thanked the Great Father for feeding and clothing us, I was really thanking God for giving us daily bread. The Dear Leader's love for the people was, in my mind, Jesus Christ's love for us. That's how I was able to remain a loyal Party member."

I was familiar with the replacement concept. He was substituting a complicated formula for a specific value in an equation. For instance, if $(x2 + 2y + 4) (x2 + 2y + 6) = 0$, the value of $x2 + 2y$ was substituted as T, making the formula $(T + 4) (T + 6) = 0$. But it didn't all make sense to me. "But you became the enemy of the people. You're an impure element."

"That is according to the Father's will."

"Which father?" I was confused now. "The Great Father?"

"No, the only Father there is. The Father in heaven. He loves us all. He sent His son into the world to wash us of our sins."

I couldn't grasp how my frail father, the Great Father, and the father in heaven were different from one another, and who among them was the father who truly loved me. "What kind of father would send his son to this world just to wash us of our sins? Someone like that couldn't possibly exist."

"Whether he exists or not isn't important," Father explained. "What's important is the belief that there's someone who loves us."

"I'd like to meet this son of his."

"We'll be able to," Father said. "You see, he's a friend of the poor, the sick, the hungry, and the oppressed."

Every time the truck halted in front of another door, more people were shoved in. Young women, old men, drowsy teenage boys, and children in arms. They smelled warm. They avoided us, as we now smelled of the cold wind. Nobody spoke or cried. Eventually the warmth in their bodies dissipated and was replaced by the smell of the abandoned. The truck continued into the black night. None of us could tell if the dark mass next to us was luggage or another person. Someone got motion sick and began to heave. Fear and anxiety dribbled from people's bodies.

HEAVEN AND ITS CONTENTS

We bounced and jostled one another as the truck rattled up an unpaved mountain road. We took in one another's faces in the dim light of dawn, at lined foreheads, sunken eyes, and broken teeth. The truck came to a halt around noon. We were at the end of the road. The sky hung low, somber and gray. People got up, their limbs stiff and their sleep-deprived eyes bloodshot.

Shabby barracks dotted the gray wasteland. Barbed wire topped the brick walls, and the dirty wooden sign said Penal Labor Colony No. 21. We were at Muryong Prison Camp— this was where political prisoners and impure elements were incarcerated. In the administrative offices, we each received a thin blanket and a single uniform. Our residence was another hour and a half into the camp. Dust bloomed on unpaved roads and clogged my throat.

Father and I were to live in a squat mud hut with a ceiling of unsecured planks. There was no electricity, and the wood-burning stove was clean, as though it had never been used. Father placed his bag on the dirt floor. The agent who accompanied us to our hut gave us our final instructions, and told us to assemble in the field when the bell rang in the morning.

The following morning, the bell sounded at five a.m. Father and I peeled our eyes open and headed to the empty field next to the huts. Pale faces bobbed about in the dark. Our area was composed of fifty or so families, creating a work crew of 170 people, who were then divided into three work units. Each cluster of households was surrounded by a four-meter-high wall crowned with an electric fence. Half a dozen work crews created one zone, and several zones made up this enormous prison camp, which encompassed a huge brick factory, a farm with an endless cornfield, an orchard, chickens and pigs, and copper and gold mines. Father was assigned to the undertaker crew. He smiled in relief.

"Hey!" a guard shouted, gesturing at Father with his baton. "What are you grinning at, asshole?"

Father froze.

Luckily for me, I was young enough to enroll in the primary school, in sixth grade; I would have been forced into hard labor had I been assigned to the middle school based on my aptitude. Classes began at eight a.m. A guard in a gray cap taught all the subjects, a baton in hand. We didn't have any Korean, math, or science books; all that was drilled into us was the history of the revolution, the Dear Leader, and ideology. The third period was devoted to preparations for work, which began in earnest in the afternoon. With our smaller hands, we were assigned to do intricate work and tasks that required us to fit in small spaces. Our lower tolerance for beatings meant that we readily followed instructions. So instead of mastering Korean, we learned how to quarry, and instead of learning English, we gathered wood for fuel. Math, physics, and chemistry were pushed aside as we reclaimed the wasteland, logged, weeded, and bred rabbits. We were divided into units of half a dozen students, based on grade and physical ability, and assigned quotas for gathering food for rabbits, fertilizing vegetable gardens with human waste, and repairing walls. The taller, stronger children were assigned the most difficult work in the quarry; they developed blisters and calluses from the large stone-filled yoked buckets they had to carry on their shoulders.

The Seven-Year Plan dictated that we sell everything that could possibly be sold overseas. We dug out anything that could be unearthed and picked anything that grew. In the spring we picked bracken and wild greens, and in the fall we picked pine mushrooms and acorns. My slowness and lack of coordination assigned me to the rabbit breeding unit. My rabbits' pelts were exported to China, and their meat went to the SPSD agents and guards. We wandered the mountains and the fields, scrounging food for the animals. We dug up the earth at the foot of mountains to haul it back to build rabbit cages. A few kids were buried under mounds of dirt in landslides and others tripped and tumbled off cliffs, but everyone was focused on how many rabbits were born and how many survived. Winter work began after the fall harvest—we repaired cages and stockpiled feed. The temperature dipped to negative 20 degrees. We began waking in the middle of the night from the cold, hunger, and pain. We were becoming translucent. At morning roll call, Father wrapped my face and hands with his uniform. A young guard had taken the gloves Jae-ha had given me. "It'll be all right," he murmured consolingly. "At least he didn't yank off your fingers."

One day, not far from the rabbit cages, a crow, its black feathers glimmering in blue and green, settled on a branch. It reminded me of a damselfly's wings. My work crew grew excited. Crows, hawfinch, and titmice that flew into the camp were snared to fill hungry bellies, prisoners plucking feathers to stuff their clothes and sharing uncooked flesh. This crow flicked its tail, taunting us. Some boys threw stones at the crow. Our determined leader, Chon Myong-sik, threw a stone that hit the branch. I jumped up, startling the crow, which looked my way before flying off, its wings gleaming. Any hope for food flew away, too. I wanted to be the bird. I wanted to fly anywhere I wished. I wanted to decide for myself whether to fly or not.

Myong-sik came up and shoved me. "It flew away because you surprised it, stupid."

I wasn't stupid, and the bird didn't fly away because of me. But my breath caught in my throat as I fell down. The other kids circled me, looking angry. The wall of faces closed in. I screamed. Someone kicked me in the gut, unleashing an avalanche of blistered hands, cracked heels, and long sticks. The world turned dark. A deep voice boomed. Everyone scattered. A rough hand wiped the blood off my mouth, but I pushed it away.

"Hey, I'm just trying to clean you up," the man said, rubbing his hand on his pants.

It was Mr. Kang, who lived with his daughter Yong-ae in the hut across from ours. I looked up. His long sideburns were flecked with white. He smiled, deep lines carving a groove in each cheek. I looked up at the sky. Where did the crow go?

Mr. Kang studied me. "I met a boy like you once. When I was living abroad."

The breeze kicked up dust, and Mr. Kang waved it away from his face. He caught me staring at his hands. Two joints were missing from his right forefinger, and his entire left pinky was gone. "Oh, this?" He grinned. "Winters took these away. Frostbite." He opened his hands to show me.

I started to think of a functional formula that calculated the length of someone's stay at a prison camp from the number of the remaining joints on his hands. "How long did it take for you to lose five joints?"

"Well, I've been digging copper for four years, now."

"Copper?"

"To get one gram of copper, you have to dig through hundred times more rock."

"Copper is a transition metal," I informed him. "It's in group eleven of the periodic table. Its atomic weight is 63.546 g/mol, its element symbol is Cu, and its atomic number is twenty-nine."

Mr. Kang nodded and looked up at the darkening sky. My eyes went to his hands again, to his asymmetrical fingers. Mr. Kang noticed my gaze and curled his fingers into fists.

"I like symmetry," I explained. "And also prime numbers and especially calculations. And formulas, geometry, equations, and sequences."

"I can tell you're a special boy," Mr. Kang remarked. "I worked for a long time at a bank, where I did the accounting. I know a bit about numbers, too."

✸ ✸ ✸

People died in the middle of the night, at dawn, and in the afternoon. They were killed by trees, smothered by a mound of dirt in the brick factory, beaten, starved, and executed. The fell off tall structures, accidentally ate poisonous plants, and succumbed to illness. Father was in charge of first aid in a hospital without any medical equipment, let alone a decent doctor. More corpses than patients came his way. A truck would pull up and someone would toss down a body wrapped in straw mats. Guards rushed forward to peel the clothes, shoes, and hat off the dead person before delivering death certificates to the next of kin, who wept quietly, the sound trickling down the paths.

"Why do they cry so quietly?" I asked Father once.

"You need energy to be sad," he whispered. "If you haven't eaten a thing, it's hard to even cry."

"Why are they crying?"

"They're crying for the dead."

I didn't think so. I was sure they were crying because they didn't want to be left behind.

Father no longer cleaned dead bodies or folded their hands neatly over their hearts. Once a fortnight, the bodies were taken to the burial site. Father and the burial team accompanied them on the back of the truck, which was covered in blood and bodily fluids. Father vomited from the motion, spitting out bitter yellow bile. Rats, plumper than people, scuttled underfoot. The corpses were light; they had been feasted on by rats and maggots. Everyone wanted to be on the burial team. They could take any rags the guards hadn't already taken and they were eligible for an extra bowl of corn noodles. One person's death became another's meal ticket. At the burial grounds, Father tossed corpse after corpse into a hole. Upon his return, he would moan all night, prostrated on the ground.

"Why don't you wipe their faces anymore?" I asked one night.

"There's no antiseptic here." Father's voice was muffled. "And there are too many deaths."

"Can they go to heaven, even with dirty faces?"

Father reached over to stroke my head, but stopped, remembering that I detested being touched. "They probably went somewhere nice, even if it isn't heaven."

"How do you know?"

"Because even hell would be better than here." Father muttered that part to himself but I heard him.

When I woke, hunger stared me down. We didn't have any food. The furnace was cold. The corn gruel Father made with half of our daily ration disappeared quickly. Father gave me two extra spoonfuls from his bowl, but that wasn't enough. Hunger dogged me. I sipped water and chewed on my tongue, which reminded me of eating meat. Pain moved in, wandering from my muscles to my bones to my joints, then to my stomach or head or ankles. The sharp, sometimes burning sensation was different from being bruised, cut, or broken.

"Hang in there," Father said. "You'll get used to it."

But I knew I wouldn't. It remained painful. I wished I were the hard winter bark of a tree. Or resolute prime numbers, firm beaks of small birds, the frozen winter ground, or the thick, yellow calluses embedded in adults' palms. They didn't feel pain, did they?

"The world you live in will be better than mine," Father said, as we walked to morning roll call. "Life will be harder, and death will multiply, but at least, as an undertaker, you won't be out of a job, no matter where you go."

Prisoners limped toward us. Father glanced at them warily and stopped speaking until they were out of earshot. "This place is hell," he muttered. "We'd be better off dead."

"What's in heaven?" I whispered.

"Everything. If anything was lacking, it wouldn't be heaven, would it?"

"So food and warmth? And Mother?"

Father nodded.

SECRETS CONCEALED IN NUMBERS

Mr. Kang was a quiet man. He never opened his mouth wide, not even when he laughed. That was because the inside of his mouth was a gold mine. He had hidden eight pieces of gold in place of his molars. I knew this because he got drunk on the strong liquor specially rationed for the Dear Leader's birthday and showed me. His mouth smelled fusty. Gold sparkled in the dark cavern of his mouth.

"You won't tell anyone, right?" He looked around. "This is all I have left. I can always pull them out and sell them. I'll be able to buy my way into something better."

"Why haven't you done it yet?"

Mr. Kang smiled faintly. "Gil-mo, never show your last hand. Only when you are at your limit do you reveal what you have."

Before coming to the prison camp, Mr. Kang had been the manager of Korea Taesong Bank's international division. Controlled by the Central Committee Bureau 39 of the Workers Party, the bank oversaw the republic's foreign currency slush fund under direction of the Dear Leader himself. Mr. Kang graduated from Pyongyang Foreign Language School and had an English degree from Kim Il-sung University. He exported coal, minerals, textiles, pottery, and medicinal herbs on behalf of the bank and imported sugar, seasoning, and household items. He also headed Korea Taesong Trading Company. Having established an account at Sberbank of Russia, Mr. Kang was hailed as a hero for bringing in foreign funds and

was appointed the head of the DPRK-UK collaboration corporation in London, where he oversaw gold and foreign currency transactions. With London as his home base, he played
a pivotal role in the foreign currency business all around
Europe, traveling to Geneva, Berlin, and Paris. Three years
into his stint, he was abruptly ordered to return. He realized
that something had gone awry. He could survive if he disre-
garded the order, but that would put his wife and daughter
back home in danger. When he landed at Sunan Airport, men
grabbed him and dragged him to the SPSD. It was all because
he had slashed the security budget of the North Korean representatives in London. His company provided funds for the
official residences throughout Europe, and he had been con-
cerned about the ballooning budget. After the fall of the USSR
and the beginning of the Arduous March, the foreign currency
situation had become dire. Though Mr. Kang had been able to
turn a profit through skilled foreign trading, there was only so
much one man could do. The only thing he could do was to
reduce the representatives' budgets. Angered, the representatives reported to their superiors in Pyongyang that Mr. Kang's
loyalty to the Party was suspect and that he was being swayed
by capitalism. After ten days of interrogation, he was ordered
to pack his bags. His family joined him on the back of a military truck.

"I knew what was waiting for me back home," Mr. Kang
confided. "I'd saved some money while I was abroad, but I
knew I'd be searched as soon as I landed in Pyongyang. So I
went to a dentist, had him pull all my molars, and replace them
with gold. I figured they wouldn't find out."

In this prison camp, he labored silently in the mines, sixteen
hours a day. Dark tunnels closed in on him as he dug along
the vein of ore, looking for copper. He believed that luck came

to those who laughed, but he never could laugh to his heart's content, afraid that the gold in his mouth would betray him. So he only laughed in the darkness underground. He laughed and laughed, thinking about what was inside his mouth. Eventually, luck heard him and came to him.

The warden of the prison camp, Yun Yong-dae, had once been the associate director of the Sinuiju SPSD, a political military officer who dreamed of making it to the Central Committee. He was discovered to be corrupt—he had been smuggling valuables from abroad—and as punishment, he was now stationed at the camp. He was determined to turn this setback into something good and demonstrate his loyalty to the Party. He figured he would return to the good graces of the Party if he could earn more foreign currency for the republic. When the warden visited the copper mine to encourage laborers to work harder, Mr. Kang went up to him and brazenly suggested that they enter into business together. He explained that he was uniquely qualified to bring in foreign currency and that he desired to head the prison camp's foreign currency work. The warden had heard all about the republic's foremost foreign currency earner; his interest was piqued.

Having escaped the death sentence of the mine, Mr. Kang was handed the books in the office. A month later, the warden ordered me to help Mr. Kang; it turned out that Mr. Kang had requested my help. We handled an ever flowing stream of numbers. The number of pine mushrooms picked by each team and their unit price; sales figures per team; output per copper mine team; the number of rabbits; the output of the brick factory and the pig farm . . . We processed primary statistics and generated precise, secondary data, such as the work team's production factor per hour; the efficiency of each work unit; the change in output of superior work units; the productivity of each individual member in each work unit; the progression of pricing of the Chinese trading company; the functional relation between the increase of production and unit price. The warden was now able to understand everything about the prison camp's money-making business in one glance. It was clear that the current productivity could increase more than 30 percent if certain measures were taken. "Could this be true?" the warden glared at Mr. Kang with suspicion.

"All we did was to extract the data, using the output and sales figures that are reported every day," protested Mr. Kang.

"I don't believe you. There's no way you can figure out the inner workings of the prison like this." The warden's Adam's apple thrummed.

"Numbers reveal our secrets," I blurted out. "If you listen carefully to what the numbers are saying, you can figure anything out."

The warden cocked his head and squinted at me.

Mr. Kang assigned me all kinds of problems. I calculated the output of each work unit per day, the unit price and amount available to be sold, and the efficiency of production. I made graphs of specific items, comparing last year's output to this year's, then predicting the output for one week, one month, and one year into the future. Based on the prediction model we came up with, Mr. Kang reported the optimal number of work units, work hours, and work methods to the warden. We analyzed the numerical value of the work for the previous three years. We discovered that working after eight p.m. decreased the total weekly output, convincing the warden to minimize late-night work. Putting more people in each work unit increased the per-person output, leading to larger teams. The warden approved all of our suggested changes.

"Gil-mo, it's a success," Mr. Kang said happily. "Math is changing the way this place is operated."

It didn't surprise me one bit. I already knew that numbers could transform anything in the world.

☆ ☆ ☆

The sunset was redder in the prison camp than the one over the Taedong River. Cornfields swelled and birds flew up; I wished Jae-ha could see this, along with the senior colonel and my math teacher. Mr. Kang was telling me about his life abroad. "People wore tight black pants, thin shirts, and ties, carefree. Their streets are lined with banks, insurance and investment companies, and people come from all around the world. They make bets and quick decisions using computers, numbers, and graphs. In those days, I would make more money in thirty minutes than this entire camp earns in one month. But sometimes I would lose that much in ten minutes."

"You should have stayed," I told him.

"I had to come back. My family. I had to return, no matter what. Pyongyang is my Ithaca, you see." Mr. Kang told me the story of Odysseus and Penelope, Agamemnon and Achilles and Hector, as well as Prince Paris, the Trojan War, and the wooden horse. I remembered some of the names from *The Possibilities of the Impossible* but didn't say anything. I had to keep my promise to the senior colonel.

"Life is a game, Gil-mo," Mr. Kang said suddenly. "You can win if you know the rules and play it well."

But hadn't he purposefully lost by returning home? "You didn't," I pointed out.

"Sometimes you have to play a game that you'll lose."

"That doesn't make sense."

"Sometimes you have to lose. Have you wondered why numbers are lined up beginning from number one? Nine is larger than one, right? But if one is smaller, why is being ranked first better than ninth?"

We started talking about beautiful sequences that could come out of those numbers. I suggested a sequence of prime numbers, but Mr. Kang said it didn't count, as it didn't include all the numbers from zero to nine. I came up with another sequence following the number of curves and straight lines that form Arabic numerals, but Mr. Kang said the rule was too arbitrary. I contemplated a few more sequences, until we came upon the most beautiful one.

"The game isn't over," Mr. Kang said. "Even though we're stuck in this camp. And it will continue until we die, maybe even after we're dead. We'll get out of here one of these days. Yong-ae will get out of here alive, I'm sure of it. When that happens, I'd like you to take care of her."

I must have looked puzzled.

"Gil-mo, you're a good person," Mr. Kang said. "A strong person can save himself, but protecting someone else is a different matter entirely. A good person has the ability to look out for someone else."

It grew windy. His long, thin frame seemed to hover, like a dragonfly.

✪ ✪ ✪

One night, as we tried to get to sleep, I turned and asked Father, "How do you think they found out about your blue book? It was hidden deep in your closet."

Father twitched in surprise, but quickly recovered. "I'm not sure."

"Someone must have told the SPSD that you were hiding it there. I think I know who."

Father stiffened. "Gil-mo, whoever it is you're thinking of, it's not that person. I'm positive."

I was hungry, and my hunger kept growing. "I can't sleep," I mumbled.

"Try counting the stars."

I counted rice kernels floating in the space of my hunger. Father began snoring. He inhaled and exhaled 126 times. I wanted to sleep—when I was sleeping, I could forget how hungry I was. Numbers floated in the darkness, then trickled down in rainbow hues. Zero was a clear raindrop, 7 was blue, 5 was reddish-brown. I stuck my tongue out to drink it. It made me want to pee. I got up quietly.

Father's bed was empty. I smelled something savory and heard a noise in the kitchen. I found Father there. "I have to pee, Father."

"Oh—yes, I do too. Let's go together." His voice was muffled.

We turned the corner of the house and stood side-by-side to pee. The white moon grew overhead.

"Tomorrow we'll receive our rations. We'll have plenty to eat," Father reassured me. He must have treated a high-level guard or SPSD agent. Or maybe he delivered a death in their family. I couldn't wait.

But the following day, Father didn't make his way home. I was called to the treatment rooms in the mortuary. Father was lying on a bed, looking up at the white, peeling exam room ceiling. "Gil-mo, promise me you'll be a good person. It's hard to be a good man, but I know you can be one."

"I will."

"Good, I'm glad." He moved, looking pained. The rusted bedsprings creaked. Then Father powered down, turning from 1 to 0. He met his death where he had delivered other deaths. I was told that he had died of acute septicemia.

Instead of Father, his portion of corn came home. On paper, he was still alive; Mr. Kang handed me the ration, and I noticed people huddled around, angling for food without an owner. They looked at me, and then at the corn I was holding.

"Your father was a great man," Mr. Kang said sympathetically. "And he made sure you would be provided for at least another three days, until the next ration."

I looked down at the 350 grams of corn Father left me. I was confused—I knew he wanted to live, to look after me, to make sure I made it out in one piece. I had figured that was why he had eaten the crusted rice last night without sharing it with me. But he had failed. Staring down at the wrinkled yellow kernels, I realized that I was alone.

✪ ✪ ✪

"Who was that awful person who informed on your father?" Angela is curious and enraged at the same time. "Who sent you and your father to the prison camp? They made it so that you don't even know where your mother ended up."

What she doesn't realize is that everyone in the republic is an informant. A father watches his children, a son spies on his mother, a wife keeps tabs on her husband. Neighbors, lovers, and colleagues are watched and informed on, so that they don't inform on you first. So it's hard to tell who informed on you. But not in this case, because I know exactly who informed on Father. "It was me."

Angela's lip twitches in surprise.

"Near the end of fall, a classmate's father passed away. He was a high-level official in the Ministry of the People's Armed Forces, and Father delivered his body. When the boy came back to school, I told him that his father was delivered to heaven so he shouldn't be sad. He grabbed me by the throat, shouting that his father wasn't a parcel. I explained to him that my father delivered the dead, telling him that you stamp the dead with a prayer to send them to heaven."

"So it wasn't you, it was him," Angela exclaims. "Your father would have known that when he was being interrogated."

"No, he didn't know. He didn't tell me he knew."

"He just didn't tell you," Angela says gently. "He didn't show that he knew."

I look down.

She places a few pages of paper in front of me. The yellow, ragged edges smell of wet dirt, the sea breeze, strong liquor, and sweat, the stench of my long voyage. She studies the symbols written on the sheets. "What are these? What is this, a code?"

"It's a language."

"What language?"

"Mine. I made it up." It's an amalgam of the languages I know—Korean, English, Russian, Chinese—and math signs and numbers. Sigma is used as a prefix, to mean adding or building something. Σenergy means cooperation or solidarity, and Σknowledge signifies refinement or knowledge. My language uses $+, -, \times, \div, \int, \doteq, \sqrt{}$ to mean something specific or, when joined with existing languages, to turn into prefixes or suffixes. I have 1,600 words, various derivatives, and a grammar system, and their location in a sentence changes their meaning.

"So what does this mean?" She's pointing to a sentence: 475 ∞ 92. It's written four times in a row.

"It means arrest." The infinity sign looks like handcuffs, and the numbers compose a simple grammar.

"Why use this complicated language when you know so many others?"

"I think the world needs a brand-new language."

Angela looks puzzled.

"I think we need a pure language," I explain. "So many words have lost their true meaning, and people cut words up and bind them together. Look at the word *hell*. The true meaning of that word has been diluted, since people use it to describe where we live now."

"So what's the use of a language that nobody else can understand?"

I hesitate.

Angela narrows her eyes. "Someone else knows it?"

I look down at the sheets of paper covered in my handwriting. I remember foxtails and dandelion seeds floating away.

"Who is it?"

"Yong-ae."

3 + 1 = 0

The first time we spoke to each other was December 12, 2000, when she came to feed the rabbits, though I knew who she was since we were neighbors. Her face contained the golden ratio of 1:1.618—the distance between her eyes to the tip of her front teeth, the length of the tip of her teeth to the point of her chin, the distance between the middle of her nose to the edge of one eye, and the length of her eyes. I raised a finger to estimate the width and length of her face. Her part was exactly at 1:1.618, and the middle of her forehead, the ridge of her nose, and the center of her chin formed that beautiful symmetry. "Your face contains the golden ratio," I blurted out.

She smiled. Her two front teeth were big, like the rabbits', and their ratio was also 1:1.618. Her shirt collar was threadbare and her shoes were holey, and her rough hands were dirty. The wind ruined the part in her hair. Unsettled by the disturbance, I reached out to smooth it in place. We walked home together. She was surprisingly frank. She said the Great Leader was an asshole and the Dear Leader killed people like he was a machine gun. We became inseparable.

One night, on our way home from the labor review session, Yong-ae showed me how to ingest light. She looked around then charged ahead, striding confidently into the darkness. Wet grass twined around our calves. She headed through the thicket, toward the slope. Pebbles slipped below our feet.

"Make sure no one's coming," she whispered. She snapped off a branch and began digging the black, wet earth. White rounds popped up. "Potatoes!" Yong-ae gathered them up and slid them down her shirt. She covered her tracks and we bounded quickly back to the path. The wind had stopped; the branches were still. The grass smelled pungent. Stars murmured and darkness grew softer as it hid us more completely. The potatoes filled our dark stomachs with light, white and warm. But the sudden ingestion of raw potatoes upset our stomachs. We visited the toilet frequently that night and darkness returned to our stomachs; hunger was our destiny.

"I wish we had rice to eat," I said. Rice was merely a concept by now, an electric storm sweeping through Uranus ten thousand years ago or territorial fights among dinosaurs. "One day I'll make sure you get to eat rice," I promised.

She held out her pinky and I hooked mine on hers.

✩ ✩ ✩

Soon, I introduced her to my language, starting with the easiest problem. I scrawled a simple expression on the ground and looked up at her expectantly.

3 + 1 = 0

She looked down at it.

"This tells the story of one gold bar and three people. It could also be written as $3P + 1G = 0$. P, of course, is people, and G is gold," I explained.

"What's the story?"

"Three thieves decide to steal a gold bar and divide it equally among themselves. They are successful and they come back to their den. They want to celebrate. One goes out to buy liquor. On his way back, he becomes greedy, and decides to poison the liquor so he can take the whole bar for himself. But when he gets back, the other two attack him. While he was out, they'd decided to kill him to divide the gold between them. They then celebrate by drinking the poisoned liquor. Then they die. A person passing by takes the gold and leaves. So in the end, nothing is left. Not the three thieves or the gold bar."

"How does this become a language?" Yong-ae looked puzzled.

"Any situation where you lose everything from greed can be described as $3 + 1 = 0$."

Yong-ae nodded, her face brightening. She learned a concept or sentence every day, and six months later, we were able to have simple conversations in Gilmoese.

✪ ✪ ✪

Yong-ae began to change—the balance and harmony in her face became more distinct as her body took on new geometric curves. Rabbits continued to grow and their pelts were delivered abroad to make clothes for people living in cold climates. Without pelts, the purplish rabbits looked smooth, and without their long ears, they looked stunted. Were soft rabbit ears hanging from coats worn by people abroad?

"The rabbits must be happier," Yong-ae muttered. "At least some part of them was able to cross the border. I wish we could leave, too."

We were in her house, making gruel out of 100 grams of corn. We finished it, but were still hungry; we waited for her father to come home. "Father was based in London," Yong-ae said. She was starting to open up to me. "I remember going to Sunan Airport when I was around eight, waving goodbye. We didn't know if he would remember us, or if he would return. He never forgot us, though. A letter would come once in a while.

Sometimes it had a dozen pencils enclosed. I'm sure many other letters were confiscated on their way to me. I started to collect the stamps on the letters he sent home." Yong-ae looked through an old wooden bag in the corner of her room, and took something out gingerly. Shiny square stamps were wrapped in thin, crackling oilpaper. They were mostly from Great Britain, with a handful from Switzerland.

"I was so impressed by them," she continued. "They brought all these heavy letters and gifts all the way home to me, you see." She picked each up and smelled it carefully.

I followed suit. They smelled slightly fishy and sweet, of a faraway world, a mysterious place. They didn't have the Great Leader or the SPSD or guards there. People probably ate white rice and beef soup anytime they wanted.

"I forgot what my father looked like eventually," Yong-ae said somberly. "I don't know if I wanted him to come back, if I'm honest with myself. But he did. We went to greet him at the airport, but we weren't allowed to see him. Then the SPSD told us to pack. We thought he was being heralded as a hero for his work in England! Maybe we were moving to a bigger house. I guess we did end up moving to a bigger house, since the camp is so big." She looked up through the gaps of the roof, at the stars. "I don't want to die here. I want to live my life."

"What would you do if you left?"

"My father told me about *The Odyssey*. He said if I read that book, I'll understand why he came back. But he didn't tell me more. As soon as I leave this place, I'm going to go to a library and read that book."

I didn't tell her that Mr. Kang had told me the story. "How will you get out of here?"

She hesitated. "When the offender dies, his family is allowed to leave," she whispered.

I knew that was why wives wished their husbands dead, and children hoped their fathers would keel over. Every night, I heard people pour out their resentments to their family members who had brought them here. "If you just died we could get out of this hellhole!" "Just go die, you asshole." "Please, Father, for us . . ." Was Mr. Kang going to die?

Yong-ae caught my worried look. She smiled bitterly. "Don't you worry," she said. "He's not an idiot. He's never going to die. If he commits suicide, he'll be buried in the streets and his family will be considered traitors. He knows that. There's no suicide in this paradise of ours."

We fell silent and stared out the window, watching a group of men walk by. They had hollow eyes and were bony, with slumped shoulders and pale, thin ankles. They seemed near death.

✪ ✪ ✪

We worked on increasingly difficult problems, trying to prove things that hadn't yet been proven. She peppered me with questions as I scribbled formulas to find the answers. "What if we added you and me?" she would ask, then wonder, "What are we going to be when we grow up?" which led to, "What are the chances we'll survive into adulthood?"

I scratched the calculations in the dirt, my numbers melding with rabbit droppings. My calculations didn't reveal any answer. Chaos disappeared and quiet filled the space around me as I kept working at them.

"So many people have died," commented Yong-ae. "But there are more and more prisoners here."

I tallied the number of families and individuals in our work unit as well as the number of work units within the prison camp. I estimated the number of prison camps in the country.

I substituted the number of people leaving from the camp with the number of people entering, calculating the rate of increase. I discovered that it would take less than twenty years for every citizen of the republic to enter a prison camp. But if people continued to die off at the same rate as they did now, it would take 128 years for the prisons to reach capacity, and more would surely be built before that happened. I explained all of that to Yong-ae. Even though I wasn't certain that she understood me and Gilmoese in our entirety, she understood enough. An expression that meant nothing to anyone else was significant for the two of us. We continued to develop our language like that.

✪ ✪ ✪

Angela glances at the pages on the desk. "So what does this say?"

"It's a letter to Yong-ae. I kept writing to her in our language so it doesn't become extinct." Does Angela realize that now half of the native speakers of Gilmoese are accused of murder? The disappearance of our language means that a world, an entire universe, is vanishing. Our collective recognition of the world, our mutual approach to life, would be lost.

"So where is she?" Angela asks.

"I don't know."

Angela narrows her eyes.

One day, Mr. Kang disappeared. He didn't come home, and he wasn't in the office. I curled up in the corner of the office, my head in my hands. After I while, I went to his desk and focused on the numbers. I finished all the calculations for the day and went to Mr. Kang's hut.

I was over there three days later when someone pounded on the door. I buried my head between my legs. The latch broke open and cold air stormed in. Men strode in without taking their shoes off and threw something heavy wrapped in straw mats on the ground. Yong-ae ran over and lifted a corner of the mat. It was Mr. Kang, his face crushed, a mangle of bloody bruises, the swelling and blood clots throwing his face off balance.

"What happened?" she screamed. "What did you do to him?"

"He's under suspicion of manipulating the books," an official snapped. "He stole the foreign currency we've all been working so hard to earn."

Instead of trying to figure out what money went where and how, they resorted to beating him. In the camp, it made no difference whether someone starved or was beaten to death. The officials walked out.

Yong-ae rushed to the kitchen to boil some water.

Mr. Kang looked around, making sure she was out of earshot. He smiled. His teeth were broken. "Gil-mo," he whispered.

"Don't forget your promise, all right? Look after her for me. Follow her wherever she goes."

"I will," I whispered back. "I'll look after her."

"Remember, Gil-mo. The game continues even after I die. So keep playing it for me. Got it?"

"I don't know what the game is," I protested.

"You do. You just don't realize it. The rules of the game are in the numbers. Remember what I told you about the most beautiful sequence in the world."

I nodded.

His eyes fluttered shut. He whispered each number, pushing them out through his throat. "9, 6, 4, 3, 0, 5, 2, 1, 7, 8."

I murmured the corresponding Korean alphabet.

"That's right," Mr. Kang said, smiling with effort. "The sequence lines numbers in order of the alphabet. Like a dictionary. And just like a dictionary, it will tell you about numbers you don't know."

Yong-ae walked in just then with a bowl of hot water. Mr. Kang struggled to open his puffy eyes. "Yong-ae, go bring the pliers from the toolbox."

"What do you need pliers for?"

"They beat me for hours but I never opened my mouth. They never found my teeth. Now you'll be able to leave this place, so take them."

Yong-ae smiled, but tears rolled down her face. She pulled out the pliers. Mr. Kang's eyes flickered and closed. We waited, but they didn't open again. He had been extinguished. Yong-ae looked down at him, her mouth set. "Come here and open his mouth," she ordered.

I pulled his jaws open. His stubble scratched my palms. Yong-ae shoved the rusty pliers in her father's mouth and extracted his gold teeth. She smiled slightly each time a gold piece emerged from his mouth. With the last gold tooth out, the inside of his mouth turned dark.

I took a wet towel and wiped Mr. Kang's face. I cleaned his swollen eyes, his bleeding forehead, his broken nose, his bloody lips, and his mangled ears. I pasted a stamp of prayer on him. His gold teeth sparkled in Yong-ae's palm. She rested her forehead on my shoulder, and I didn't mind. Her forehead became heavier and heavier, and then began to heave. My shoulder grew warm and wet.

Around noon the following day, three SPSD agents descended on us. They had come on bicycle. Workers from the undertaker unit shoved Mr. Kang into a wheelbarrow and carted him away. We were ordered to each get on the back of a bicycle. The agents began to pedal. Spokes spun, sunlight bouncing off them. We rattled down the stony path. Thirty minutes later, we arrived at the SPSD offices, and we were taken to the warden's office.

"Comrade Kang Chi-u acknowledged his mistakes during our interrogations," the warden told us. "Thanks to the mercy of the Dear Leader, the family is released when the offender dies. Comrade Kang Yong-ae, you're free to go."

A smile rippled across Yong-ae's face.

"Comrade Ahn," the warden addressed me. "You have quite a talent for numbers. You are now in charge of the books."

Was this the game Mr. Kang mentioned?

"Was my father really guilty?" Yong-ae asked cautiously.

The warden nodded. "He was very calculating, your father. He was very good. Our earnings increased threefold based on his recommendations. But then, he went too far. He had separate books and funneled a portion of the sales for himself. Comrade Ahn helped him manage the accounts, but he had no idea what was going on. You just did as you were told, didn't you?" The warden looked at me.

I didn't answer.

"We found duplicate books detailing what he had siphoned over a year and a half. I was going to look the other way if he confessed, because he was so important to our foreign currency project. But he refused to talk. He only acknowledged his role after he was beaten, but he never said where the money went. What would he do with all that money, anyway? His efforts have been noticed by the Central Committee. I'm sure I'll be given a different post soon. If he weren't so stubborn, we would have seen better times together . . ." The warden trailed off.

✪ ✪ ✪

That night, we sat in her house in the dark. Cold starlight filtered in through the gaps in the ceiling. Her eyes glistened. "I wish we could leave together."

I did, too. "Where will you go?"

"Musan. Then I'm going to cross into China."

"I will, too. I'll be right behind you."

Yong-ae took a small photograph of herself from her bag and handed it to me.

The next day, she left the camp. It was as if she had vanished. Everything was now dark and dreary. All day long, I talked to myself in Gilmoese. People murmured that I had gone mad.

The warden pushed books filled with numbers toward me. They beckoned. I added and subtracted, multiplied and divided, and found the square root and the log value. I calculated the output, unit price, and production rate of each work unit. The warden pulled the books toward him and grinned. He placed them in his office and handed me warm corn cakes. I stuffed them in my mouth. I was so hungry. He poured me some water. He promised me more corn cakes if I kept calculating like this.

He tossed three small books in front of me. "Take a close look at these numbers," he said. "I think you'll find interesting things."

The books were filled with Mr. Kang's familiar, distinctive hand. He wrote the European way, crossing his sevens and zeros. Nobody in the republic wrote this way. "Are these Mr. Kang's secret books?" I asked.

The warden shook his head. "No, he created these books for each item. You'll be able to figure it out quickly. These have to be maintained every day. Remember, you'll get corn cakes every day if you perform well."

I worked hard, the numbers bumping and mixing together as they entered my head, revealing the output and unit price of specific items. Not too long after, I put my pencil down. "The sum of all 523 numbers is 1,274,690."

The warden picked up the books.

"Why was I not freed after my father died?" I blurted out.

The warden looked at me appraisingly. "Comrade Kang suggested that he would watch over you and have you help him with the accounting. He said there was nowhere for you to go, and that you wouldn't be able to survive out there alone. That's why I decided to keep you on."

"Why am I not freed now? Mr. Kang's dead, too."

"It would be too cruel to send you out into the world," the warden explained gently. "You're all alone. You don't have anyone who could help you."

Every day, I went into the office to poke around in the world of zeros and sevens and other numbers Mr. Kang left behind. My stomach was full for the first time in a long while thanks to the corn cakes, but my heart gaped from Yong-ae's absence. My feet stopped still whenever I thought of her. Everything turned to zero when I multiplied it by her. I kept thinking of Mr. Kang

asking me to look after her. I was breaking my promise to him
for corn cakes.

❀ ❀ ❀

I didn't escape the prison camp, not exactly. I didn't hatch a
plot; I didn't even have a plan. I just left.

Two months after Yong-ae's departure, the warden handed
me another book. "There's definitely something strange about
this book," he told me. "Figure it out."

I didn't find anything odd about the calculations. Even if
there were something that didn't quite line up, Mr. Kang
wouldn't have made it easy to find. The warden was frustrated
and threw the book aside. That was when I noticed something
purple stuck to the back. It was a Swiss stamp from Yong-ae's
collection. I had to get it back to her; it was rightfully hers.

That night I put my belongings in my worn knapsack. I
added the corn cake I had saved from earlier and the book
of Mr. Kang's calculations I had slid into my pocket when the
warden wasn't looking. I walked toward the entrance to the
camp. Darkness shattered underfoot. Guards made continuous rounds and electricity crackled through the barbed wire
fence around the perimeter. I walked up to the guard post at the
entrance. A beam of light made me freeze. I shaded my eyes. I
heard the click of rifle. "Hey, it's the idiot," the guard called.
"Where are you going in the middle of the night?"

"I have to deliver this ledger," I said.

The guard pursed his lips and conferred for a long time with
the shift lead. "You're delivering a ledger this late at night? The
warden's asked you to do this?"

I just stared up at the watchtower. Finally, the head guard
called down to another guard; nobody felt that he could call

the warden in the middle of the night to confirm. "Take him into town!"

I got on the back of a bicycle. The guard pedaled hard, panting. Each push of the pedal brought one exhale and three-quarters of a rotation of the wheel, which had a diameter of 66.04 centimeters. One breath and one pedal pushed the bicycle 1.55 meters forward. The guard's back grew damp. I thought about Poincaré's conjecture. In 1904, Poincaré asked, "Consider a compact three-dimensional manifold V without boundaries. Is it possible that the fundamental group of V could be trivial, even though V is not homeomorphic to the three-dimensional sphere?" If we had a long cord, we could determine the shape of Earth without having to go into outer space to look down at it. You could secure one end of the cord to a single place and hold the other as you circled the earth; by the time you were back to the starting point, you could hold each end of the cord in either hand, creating a loop around the equator. You could pull on it, making the loop shrink until the whole cord is back in your hands, demonstrating that we do, in fact, live on a sphere.

But if the earth were shaped like a donut, you wouldn't be able to retrieve the long cord; it would either stay on the inner circumference or be wrapped around one part.

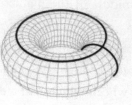

Thinking about Poincaré's conjecture reassured me. I knew I would be able to see Yong-ae again. Earth is a sphere; she had left our point on Earth, but we were connected by an invisible cord. If I could follow that cord, I would meet up with her.

DAY THREE: *KKOTJEBI*
March–September 2002

Soldiers marched stiffly along the still, gray streets, past the crumbled walls, slumped people, and emaciated rats scurrying through holes in the walls. The dead and the dying lay in rotting gutters amid broken telephone poles. I stamped them with a short prayer. Electrical wires were draped so low that they nearly grazed the top of my head. I heard murmurings, sounds of a tussle, then shouts. I turned the corner and found myself in a market where vendors were selling fistfuls of rice; a few eggs; lettuce, cucumbers, and eggplants grown in their gardens; a mound of wild greens; hand-knit scarves and gloves; and Chinese-made buckets and pots, all on low display stands lining the narrow street. It seemed that people were selling anything they could get their hands on. The stands went for one, two, or five won, depending on the size, and grasshoppers—those who didn't have enough to even rent a stand—sold their wares on the ground. The air was dense with arguments.

"Camp guards!" someone shouted, and the market erupted. Merchants packed up their goods and fled down the alley, upending display stands. Something heavy hit the back of my neck and I fell to the ground. Muddy, holey shoes began kicking me. I spotted some bare callused feet, some missing pinky toes. I plugged my ears and screamed. A rough hand twisted my arm. They had found me already. I had left the camp only yesterday. Suddenly, my back was lighter, and the beating stopped.

"My bag!" I yelped, realizing they weren't guards, they were thieves. I looked around. In the chaos of shouting people and crying children, patrols were blowing their whistles, and I spotted a thin man dashing away with my knapsack. I ran after him. He scurried through the narrow alleys and a maze of empty huts, crumbled walls, and smelly sewers. My legs were wobbly. The thief led me around the neighborhood, as I began understanding the structure of the maze—two dead ends and three exits. I darted down a shortcut. The man was at a dead end, and I was now blocking his only exit. He turned around, panting. He wasn't a man at all. He must have only been sixteen or seventeen, his hair shaggy and overgrown.

"It's mine," I mumbled.

He threw my knapsack at me, and I backed up, my hands outstretched, trying to follow the arc of my bag. It landed on the ground. A gang of small, thin, dirty kids, ranging from eight to nineteen years old, approached from the other side. One stood at the entrance to the alley and let out two long whistles and one short one, which caused everyone to run to a government building at the end of the alley and open the broken glass doors. Inside was a man with long sideburns sitting in a chair.

"We have a very important guest, I see," he called out. He straightened his shabby suit jacket and sliced the air with his hands. The kids instantly split to either side of him, their backs against the wall.

He threw me a cold glance as he rummaged through my knapsack. He took a bite of the corn cake I'd saved and threw my bag to the side. "Where did you come from, the prison camp? If Dash hadn't taken this useless bag of yours, you would have been taken back and hanged. Get over here, Dash!"

The thin boy approached and was greeted by a vicious kick to the chest. He flew a short distance and fell to the ground. I estimated the distance, the speed, and the arc of his flight and calculated the amount of pain he must have experienced.

"What's wrong with you?" snapped the man. "You take this stupid bag, of all things, and get caught by this kid?"

Dash's white, blistered lips were now crimson. "I didn't get caught," he mumbled. "He knows this alley. He was standing at the exit."

The man snorted. "I've never seen this kid before. How would he know this place better than you?"

I went to my knapsack, took out a nub of pencil, and drew the diagram of the alleys in my notebook.

The man's eyes bulged. "How do you know this area so well?"

I didn't answer.

A grin crept over the man's face. "Hey, Dash, you did good. You brought back something very interesting." He tossed the boy the remaining bits of corn cake.

Dash leaped up to grab the crumbs, then savored them slowly. When he swallowed, all the kids, who had been watching his mouth intently, swallowed in unison.

"Dash, teach this kid properly, all right?"

Looking pleased, Dash wiped the blood off his lips with his grimy sleeve. Everyone looked at him with envy.

✪ ✪ ✪

We were known as *kkotjebi*, which literally meant "flower swallow." In Russian, though *kochev'ye*, meant nomad or wanderer. A beautiful thing in one language became something tragic in another. We orphans roamed the streets, rummaging through trash, scrounging for spoiled food, eating grass, begging, and stealing. *Kkotjebi* like us lived all across North Korea, with a strong concentration near the Chinese border, moving often in groups for ease of survival.

People had abandoned the maze of alleys we hung out in after an outbreak of typhoid fever two years ago. Our leader, whom we called Straw Cutter because of his violent tendencies, oversaw our activities and deployed us to various parts of town. Under Straw Cutter's orders, Dash shadowed me. Or was it that I followed him around? Either way, he watched me but I also received his protection. "Just do as I say," he counseled early on in our partnership. "When I say run, you run. When I say hide, you hide. Understand?"

When the merchants saw us approaching, they shooed us away, but we retreated before going back, persistently. We would do anything if it meant we could eat. Even though he himself had tried to steal my knapsack, Dash solemnly introduced me to the code of conduct. "We're not thieves, remember. Don't take something from someone. This is how you do it, okay?" He got up, his eyes focused. He sneaked up to a display stand across the way, bumping deliberately into a woman haggling with the shopkeeper over the price of sorghum cake; she dropped the cake in surprise when she was jostled, and Dash ducked, grabbed the cake, and shoved part of it in his mouth as he darted away. "Go!" he hissed.

I scampered after him blindly. Eventually, we came to a stop, panting, and leaned on a secluded wall.

"See?" Dash said. "We don't steal. I didn't steal this from that woman. All we do is pick things up when people drop or throw them away. That's not a crime." He grinned, showing me his broken front teeth, and tore off a small piece of sorghum cake. He handed it to me. Dirt and grit covering the cake crunched between my teeth, and it tasted nutty. The cake disappeared into our gullets, and that one piece shook awake the hunger within. We went back to the other side of the market. Straw Cutter would be waiting for us at sundown, expecting us to bring him food we procured. We rummaged through the trash to pick out things that might be edible, but all we could find were a desiccated outer leaf of a cabbage and a corncob.

"If he finds out we ate the sorghum cake, he'll kill us," Dash warned.

We shoved each other as we leaped over puddles. When we got back, Straw Cutter and the other kids beat us just shy of death for not bringing anything back. Beatings and hunger were inversely proportional, I thought.

🛡 🛡 🛡

One day, we clambered into the forest, thick with exotic smells, colors, and silence. Hunger swelled in us, making us want to eat decomposing leaves, tough pieces of bark, and unfamiliar mushrooms.

"You can die if you eat the wrong thing," Dash said. "But if you're lucky, you won't die, you'll just get to have a full belly. There are tons of things to eat here." He looked around excitedly.

The buzz of bees ferrying pollen surrounded us as water trickled between mossy rocks toward the waterfall on the other side of the valley. I thought I could hear the footsteps of ants as they scurried in and out of a rotting log. Dash crept forward, his bare, cracked heels stained green from the vegetation underfoot. He stopped and pointed at a bramble bush. Wild strawberries glimmered through the green leaves. Dash picked a fruit and handed it to me. It burst in my mouth. We dove at the bush, stuffing our faces. The sun warmed our skin. Thorns became embedded in our palms and scratched the backs of our hands, but we didn't care. Finally, we flopped on our backs in the knee-high grass. Red juice stained our fingers, lips, tongue. Red, tart stars twinkled in our mouths. Why did hunger return so quickly? Why did we get hungry in the first place? Yellow pollen clung to legs of bees that buzzed past our heads. The breeze weaved through the grass. Our stomach muscles stretched out, loosening; the tart juice rumbled through and formed gas, and the sound exploded out of us.

Dash giggled, grabbing his stomach. "Long time no see! I've forgotten what it's like to fart."

We laughed, passing gas with each guffaw. We pulled our pants down to take a shit on a low hill. The sky was touching our behinds as the grass tickled our backs. Our shit was speckled with small red seeds.

The sun set. Our red lips and hands would reveal our clandestine activity. Dash sucked the tips of his stained fingers and grinned. "Let's go. At least we'll be full when Straw Cutter beats us."

Back home, Straw Cutter made us get down on all fours and used a big stick to beat us. Each time the stick made contact with my back, I licked my lips for the tart taste of wild berries. Next to me, Dash twisted in pain, tears flowing down his face. That night, I dreamed of a multihued world filled with wild strawberries.

✪ ✪ ✪

Fists ruled the market—merchants chased away the grasshoppers, who threatened us with clubs. Merchants, for their part, kowtowed to the senior patrol, who sniveled to the SPSD. When the SPSD appeared, everyone scattered. From our hiding place around the corner, Dash would peek at the SPSD agents stomping around in polished leather shoes. "They actually help us work the market," he whispered. "Straw Cutter pays them off once a month so we can sell things that come from the camp, like vegetables and wild greens. We hand off pine mushrooms and rabbit pelts to smugglers, and they take it across the border. If you upset them, you can't stay around anymore. That's why merchants and grasshoppers who don't buy their wares or miss rent disappear the very next day. Everyone knows that we're close to the SPSD, so that's how we can pretty much do whatever we want here."

The patrol, however, still flexed their muscles when the SPSD weren't around. They took our dirty rice cakes and puny steamed corn and tiny rotting potatoes, threatening us with clubs. After one incident, Dash offered me his sleeve as I spat blood out of my mouth. "Just give them what they want," he advised. "They'll take it whether they beat you for it or you give it up. Assholes. I wish we could unleash the SPSD at them."

But we had to keep a low profile; if the SPSD got involved, they might figure out that I'd escaped from the camp. When the patrol took my things, I poked through the trash until it was late. That meant Dash had to stay with me and help; if he went back alone, Straw Cutter would be incensed that he left me behind; if we went back together with nothing, he would also get a beating for bringing nothing home.

"I wish I were in the prison camp," Dash grumbled, rubbing his sore ass after a beating one night. "I'd go anywhere to get three hundred fifty grams of corn a day."

"No, you don't. And anyway, we have to find Yong-ae," I told him.

"Who's this Yong-ae?"

I took out a picture of Yong-ae from my shirt pocket. In the photograph, she was wearing a dark school uniform, wearing her hair parted in the middle. "She said she was going to cross the Tumen."

Dash stared at me. "Cross the Tumen? That's an act of betrayal to the republic and the Dear Leader! Border guards will shoot you without warning. And a girl crossing alone?" He shook his head, looking troubled. "Are you in love with her?"

What did it feel like to love someone? I did like doing things for her.

"Don't bother looking for her," Dash continued. "She's probably done for."

"Like she's dead?"

"Well—for a girl . . ." he trailed off.

We were each in our own space and time. If I could fold time, if I could bend space, we would meet at a point in the universe. I had to find her somehow.

✪ ✪ ✪

Not long after, we were all hanging out in an abandoned building when Straw Cutter came up to Dash. "Keep the idiot close," he said, ignoring me completely. "He's valuable."

"Don't worry about it," Dash said lazily. "He's not going anywhere."

Straw Cutter slapped him across the cheek. Dash crumpled to the ground. Straw Cutter ripped a page out of *Review of Revolution* and rolled a cigarette using stolen tobacco leaves. He blew bluish smoke into Dash's face. "Listen up. The kid's an unripe plum. Do you understand? When we find this girl and hand both of them over, we'll get a reward that's three times larger. Don't lose him, now, okay?" He took out a photograph and flashed it.

Dash wiped the blood off his face and squinted at the photograph.

"The warden wants to capture this girl along with the kid. They were in the camp together. When she left, apparently that's when the kid broke away, trying to go after her. The warden really needs him, but since he'll keep following the girl, he won't leave again if the two of them are together. Who knows why he needs this dummy? Watch him closely. He must know something about where the girl went."

The other kids gathered around to study the picture, which was handed from dirty hand to dirty hand. Straw Cutter snatched it away before it got to me. "All right, everyone remember her face. Come right to me if you see her anywhere."

A couple of older kids murmured among themselves. Straw Cutter's eyes flashed angrily at them. A mustachioed kid nervously piped up. "I think I've seen her at the market."

Straw Cutter shoved the kids aside to get to him. "When?"

"A few months ago. I went to the Chinese peddler to sell rabbit pelt. I saw her there." The boy hesitated.

Straw Cutter motioned for him to continue.

"She looked older than the picture, but she couldn't have been more than sixteen or seventeen. She was wearing makeup and tight clothes, and she was flirtatious. The peddler was leering at her."

Straw Cutter grimaced. "So she sold something."

"What was she trying to buy?" asked the boy, puzzled.

"She must have already crossed the Tumen. Those peddlers can cross any time, because they bribe the border guards. They certainly could cross with a girl like that if they wanted to." Straw Cutter crossed his arms in anger and turned around.

I studied his worn wristwatch, counting my heartbeat. One hundred twenty-three times a minute. She was here a few months ago. In the very market I roamed every day. But she was no longer here.

✧ ✧ ✧

Rats clambered along the ceiling rafters. They became dogs with burned-off tails in my dreams. She walked among them, wearing a fluttery yellow dress. I walked along behind her, watching the sunlight slide down her curls. Her shoulders squirmed and sprouted wings, which broke through her thin dress. She flapped her wings. The breeze was warm. She was standing on a tall cliff now, and she flew up, entrusting herself to the wind. Yong-ae, I called. I don't have wings. I leaped off the cliff after her, but I fell at the rate of 9.8 m/s^2. Was I going to die?

Someone shook me. "Wake up, Gil-mo."

My eyes flew open. I stopped falling.

"Pack your things," Dash whispered. "We have to leave. Now."

I flung my knapsack over my back and crept out of our hut behind him. A Jeep was parked in front of Straw Cutter's hut.

"He called for you," Dash said, pulling my sleeve to get me to move. "The warden is here. Straw Cutter wants to hand you over."

Outside, we became one with the darkness. We skirted behind Straw Cutter's hut, peeking inside through a crack in the wall. Straw Cutter was taking out a bundle of dollars from his inner pocket to hand to the warden. The warden counted each bill and put it in his pocket.

"I have the kid you're looking for," Straw Cutter said ingratiatingly. "I sent for him. I couldn't get both him and the girl, but I'm sure you'll still be generous."

"Bring him now!" snapped the warden.

Straw Cutter's lip twitched.

"Run, Gil-mo," whispered Dash. "If we're caught, we're dead."

We sprinted toward the hill behind the maze of alleys. Darkness slammed into our faces as overgrown weeds scraped our legs and tree branches whipped our heads. We were out of breath by the time we made it to the top of the hill. The wind threw itself at us as we looked down. The warden's Jeep turned on, the headlights bright against the night. We could hear Straw Cutter's annoyed voice and kids being woken up to look for us. We slid down into soft, slick darkness on the other side of the hill.

"Speed is proportional to gradient and inversely proportional to friction," I informed Dash as we scooted down.

We tumbled into mud. Venomous insects bit us. Blisters grew and burst, and we slept in the gutters and stumbled on. We headed toward the Tumen River, stepping over the dead pebbling the streets, collapsed against walls and crumpled over in crumbling staircases. I pasted stamps of prayers on them when I could.

As we made our way toward the Tumen, Dash told me more about himself than he ever had. He wanted to be a novelist—his stories would be something nobody had ever even imagined. He would shock the world, he vowed, with his sad but hilarious and beautiful but frightening novel. You would root for his characters, but you would also secretly hope that they be placed in great danger, and you would be devouring the book but wishing that it would never end. Our voyage would be the basis of his great novel. When he talked about his future, he turned suddenly youthful and full of hope.

We ran along the bumpy unpaved road overgrown with weeds and carved with puddles. We moved constantly, away from the warden and Straw Cutter. When we became hungry we collapsed and slept, and when we woke we staggered to our feet to walk on. We didn't even have dreams, as that required energy. We floated along in our dreamless sleep.

One day, we woke to two gruff soldiers poking us with the muzzles of their guns. Both were skinny, though one was tall and the other short. Neither looked older than twenty. "Where are you from?" snapped the short one. "Take out your passes."

We of course didn't have travel passes. A look of momentary panic flashed across Dash's face.

The tall soldier glanced at me as I gaped at them. "This one looks a little slow."

"Oh, him? He's a math genius," rambled Dash. "He went to Pyongyang First Middle School according to a special order by the Dear Leader. He went to the Math Olympiad as a representative of the republic." He began rummaging through my knapsack, messing everything up.

I plugged my ears and screamed.

Dash took out my thick notebook filled with formulas. "See? He's been researching this for the past year. Topology problems. He solved it, even though nobody else in the entire world has."

The tall soldier glanced at his shorter colleague.

"We're on our way home, to Musan. But we got lost." Dash sounded pitiful.

The short soldier snorted. "You're in Musan. What kind of idiots look for Musan when they're standing there?"

Dash grinned widely and bowed repeatedly. He started to walk away rapidly, dragging me along.

We crouched and looked at the Tumen River through the long grass. The Taedong River back home drew young lovers, sunburned boys, and flocks of doves, surrounded by deep-rooted willows. The Tumen attracted fleeing men and women, soldiers who shot them, and the dead that sank in the water, carried off by the current and nibbled on by the fish. We crawled along the river, hidden in the grassy bank. A plastic bag flew toward us across the span. I picked it up and wrapped my knapsack in it. We reached the shallows around sunset.

Tar-painted guard posts stood sentry every thirty meters. Soldiers hitched their AK-47s over their thin shoulders, patrolling the space between the posts every ten minutes. We stayed put until it got dark. Every so often, a body floated down, its belly swollen, pale, and translucent.

Dash pounded on his calves, which had become numb. "When the guards head back to the post, we're going to sprint across, okay? If we make it to the water, we're halfway there."

At his signal, we darted through the grass. The river flexed its black scales, pitching violently. We hesitated. The guards were about to turn around to return to the first post. Dash clenched his eyes shut and pushed me down the slope. He leaped down after me. We landed on the muddy bank. The river opened its glistening eyes, deep, cold, and mysterious. It screamed with a million small, shiny tongues. Dash tore his clothes off. He pulled mine off, too. "Let's go!" he hissed. He tied one end of his belt to my wrist and the other to his own. The river writhed. It was cold and slippery. We inched forward. Halfway across, the water swelled and threw me down. I began to float away. Was I dying? Where was it taking me? I sank. I floated up again. I glimpsed twinkling stars. Water and darkness rushed into my eyes and mouth. My stomach grew full. Eventually, the growling river stopped thrashing and glided through the grass. Dash flailed his arms, throwing up water and words together. "We're almost there! We made it across!" The river had sucked us in, held us, then spat us onto the opposite bank. It settled quietly to sleep.

DAY THREE: YANJI
September 2002–February 2003

B anks tosses a stiff document stamped with the red official seal of the Chinese government in front of me and leaves. Apparently this proves that I am a member of a fearsome criminal organization and an illegal immigrant.

Re: Jiang Jiajie, Drug Carrier, Yanji
—Beijing Municipal Bureau of Public Security

Jiang Jiajie is a North Korean refugee who illegally entered China via the Tumen River in September 2002. Operating from his base at a Yanji brothel, Jiang was part of a drug ring in the northeast, in charge of transporting vast quantities of smuggled drugs from North Korea to major cities throughout China. In February 2003, he fled to Shanghai, eluding the Jilin Provincial Bureau of Public Security's investigation.

Angela spoons pumpkin soup into my mouth. The pain in my leg has diminished 20 percent since yesterday. She pricks my arm with a sharp needle. The used syringe clatters on the tray.

"They've confirmed your dragon tattoo to be the emblem of the Fierce Dragon Society, the criminal organization based in northwest China." Angela studies my face.

My body is my life's ledger, retaining all the things I have done. The scent of lavender and the stench of a burning corpse are seared into my nose, and the sensation of an empty belly is always with me. Ugly things are carved on me. But perhaps ugly things can ultimately create beauty.

"I have a functional formula for the relationship between freedom and weight," I tell her. To begin talking about the dragon tattoo, I have to start with what happened in Yanji. Freedom.

We walked along the ditch on the other side of the Tumen, dripping with water. By the time our clothes dried, we spotted lights. Yanji. There were fewer soldiers and more women than we were used to, and of course, everything was in Chinese. All these changes meant nothing for us, as we were still hungry. Even the trash heaps were more plentiful in Yanji, filled with food, torn newspapers, water-logged magazines, empty packs of Lucky Strike, and user manuals for South Korean color televisions. Thanks to the hours I put in combing through the trash in Yanji, I knew how to work a color television before ever owning one, and I was familiar with the American surgeon general's warning on cigarette packs before setting foot on American soil.

A few days later, a balding man with a symmetrical moustache and goatee came up to us in the trash heap. "You crossed the Tumen, didn't you?" the man asked in Korean, pulling at his moustache.

I ignored him. Dash perked up. "We're from Musan," he said. "Nice to meet you."

The man's eyes darted around. He slapped Dash on the head. "Don't speak in Korean," he hissed. "There are SPSD agents all around here. They're disguised as defectors. They ferret refugees out and take them back. It's better to be mute if you don't know Chinese."

Dash turned pale. He murmured, "I thought we were safe here."

"It isn't safe anywhere if you're a defector," the man admonished.

Dash lowered his head.

The man shook his head and placed his hand on Dash's shoulder. "Do you have a place to go?" he asked, somewhat sympathetically.

Dash shook his head. The man gestured to the end of the alley, where an old but well maintained Toyota was waiting. "Get in, then. You'll be able to avoid the SPSD if you do as I say."

We drove through a busy red-light district. It was still early in the evening but the streets were raucous, neon lights flashing and drunks weaving around. Bare skin flared in garish lights, heels clacked on the pavement, and laughter rang out. We entered a building with a flashing neon sign, bigger and larger than any other: it cycled through 장백산, Changbaishan, and ┌白山. We were led down a long corridor before going downstairs. Our guardian opened the steel door at the end of the hallway to a room filled with big men in suits. The men bowed.

Dash looked around warily.

"You'll work here," our savior told us, then turned and disappeared upstairs.

The men in suits glared at us.

Dash smiled ingratiatingly. "Who is that?"

"What's the date today?" asked one man.

"September 18, clear then overcast," I mumbled.

The man ignored me. "Remember this date," he said haughtily. "Meeting Zheng Hanmo was the luckiest thing that could ever happen to you." He explained that Zheng was the owner of Changbaishan, the leading entertainment house in all of

Yanji. "He operates four upscale entertainment complexes here, and has the liquor distribution rights for the area. Not even the simplest task can be done without his involvement. His influence reaches not only our bureau of public security but also the SPSD along the border."

A larger man cut him off. "Put your belongings in that cabinet over there and change into your uniforms."

We were to wash dishes, clean up, and bring customers in off the street. Stationed in the street, Dash grinned at me. "We've just got on the back of a tiger," he said. "We should probably be screaming at the top of our lungs."

I didn't know what he meant.

We woke at four in the morning every day. We took a cart to the market to help ferry vegetables, fruit, meat, and seafood into the kitchen. It would be past ten by the time we finished cleaning the kitchen and washed and trimmed the produce for the day. After a quick lunch, we vacuumed the hallway and wiped down tables. Dash pulled on rubber gloves to plunge toilets plugged with cigarette butts and vomit. "Here we are, cleaning up shit," he groused. "And to think, we managed to escape!" Even though he complained, he was content. He grew wider and rounder, his appetite insatiable. He stuffed leftover food in his mouth. Was he trying to track down and eat all the meals he had skipped? He didn't care what it was—bar snacks and food discarded by customers, vegetable peels, cold rice, flat beer—if it could be ingested, it went straight into his mouth. In the first month he gained five kilograms. Two weeks later, he gained another three. Fat plumped his eyelids and cheeks and filled the curve between each rib, the nubs of his spine, and the space between his wrist bones and fingers. He became a completely different person in three months. He was only fifty-three kilograms when we were in Musan, and now he was nearly eighty kilograms. He looked happily at the spot where his ribs used to protrude from his chest. He wasn't fast or agile like his namesake anymore; he was fat, wiping sweat pooled between the folds on his neck. His quick tongue was the only thing that remained the same. "I feel alive when I feel my body expanding," Dash announced as he made the toilet sparkle. As the afternoon waned, we hit the streets to coax men into the establishment. While Dash waddled over to our targets and worked his persuasive tongue, I stared blankly into the distance.

After dark, Dash changed into black pants and a white shirt with a bowtie straining against his neck, and walked the hall, a tray in hand. I wore an apron, washing glasses and plates streaming into the kitchen. When guests left at the end of the night, Dash tackled the dishes I didn't manage to get to, and we would finish up around two in the morning.

Dash chomped on the snacks he had pocketed from the tables. "I love it here," he crowed. "We never go hungry! Do you wonder what it would be like to go to a real capitalist country like America? I'd become rich. I love money." He took out gold-rimmed glasses that a drunk customer had left behind. "What do you think? Don't I look like a wealthy intellectual?"

What did a wealthy intellectual have to do with a discarded pair of glasses?

Dash took out a one-dollar bill he had secreted in his pants pocket and smoothed it open. He put his nose to it and inhaled, then kissed George Washington.

I went back to thinking about Yong-ae. Someone would have spotted her if she had gone through this area. She would have spoken to someone. Even an animal leaves footprints.

Later, we stepped into the streets. Neon lights were turning off, one by one. Dash was at home in the narrow streets glistening with lights and bubbling with female laughter. He politely greeted large men wearing fedoras and black suits swaggering around, calling them "Mister." Dash looked enviously at their wide shoulders as they roamed the alleys in packs. "I want to be in a gang," he said wistfully. "I need to get bigger."

"Why do you want to be in a gang?"

"Nobody bothers you if you're a gang member." He stared enviously at a group of men who turned the corner and disappeared. He imitated their strut as we walked into a bar at the end of the alley. Wearing a sullen expression, he ordered a bowl of spicy soup and a bottle of South Korean soju in a husky voice.

The bar was bursting with women in heavy lipstick and short skirts. He appraised the girls over his gold-rimmed glasses. His glasses and girth added five or six years to his appearance. "Hey, Miri!" he called, approaching a neighboring table. "How did you do today? Good tips?"

Miri downed a glass of *soju* and waved him off. He jumped back, grinning. Miri laughed despite herself. Women usually liked Dash's gift of gab and his easy laughter, but they couldn't be bothered with a boy with no money.

I looked around. I spotted a woman with tangled hair drinking by herself at a two-person table near the entrance. I brought over Yong-ae's photograph, which had gotten wet on my journey across the Tumen. "Have you seen this girl?" I asked nervously. "She's my friend. I'm looking for her."

The woman glanced at the photograph and kept drinking. "A pretty girl like that? She would have left this place already. This city is crawling with guys who'll do whatever it takes to make some money. You think they'd leave a pretty young thing like that alone? I bet she got sold off somewhere."

"Where?"

"How should I know? It's a big country."

✪ ✪ ✪

As I suspected, Yong-ae had left her traces in town, at a small
bar, as well as at a dance hall and a lounge. Her name changed
at each establishment, but everyone remembered her clearly.
Men recalled her bad accent and charming smile, smiling with
a faraway look in their eyes. One bar owner showed us an
IOU Yong-ae had written, insisting that we pay her debt. Dash
reassured the owner that she had ripped us off too, which was
why we were looking for her. The owner handed over a crumpled thousand-yuan note. "She probably went to another club.
Come find me when you get her. I swear I'm going to put her
in prison." Dash reiterated our trustworthiness. I watched him,
realizing he could never be a menacing gangster; he smiled too
much.

THE PROBABILITY OF ONE MAN AND
ONE WOMAN FALLING IN LOVE

Late one night, on the 128th day since we crossed the river, Dash took me to a bar. He had heard that the owner of this bar was a madam who had been very powerful at one point. Everyone called her Mama. When we got there, we found a chubby woman in her forties in a red polka-dot blouse and a dark purple skirt. I showed her Yong-ae's photograph. Mama studied it with sleepy eyes. "Must be an old picture. She's in a school uniform. Their faces change quickly here. Anxiety takes away a girl's beauty." Her lashes looked heavy.

I tried to imagine Yong-ae wearing fake eyelashes and red lipstick like Mama. "She came across the Tumen," I confided. "I have to find her."

"This place is crawling with girls who came over," Mama scoffed. "They stay around until the SPSD catches them. If they're lucky, they hide out somewhere, but they're often sold by human traffickers. Don't moon over a girl," she advised. "Concentrate on how you're going to survive." She drank a cup of cold *soju*.

Where could she have gone? I hunched over and covered my ears.

"Don't be discouraged," she said gently. "You'll find her, I'm sure."

I removed my hands from my ears. "How?"

"Of all the possibilities, the likelihood of a boy and a girl meeting and falling in love and the chances of them parting are the lowest. And a boy and a girl are most likely to fall in love, fall out of touch, then meet again, apparently. I don't know how that's possible, but there you have it."

Mama didn't relate the theory accurately, but I recognized the idea. After all, I had told Yong-ae in Gilmoese about these probabilities and we had worked on long, complicated calculations to prove them. "You know Yong-ae!" I leaned forward. "Where is she?"

She waved a hand. "I don't know any Yong-ae."

"This girl." I shoved the photograph in her face.

She snorted and topped her glass. "That's not Yong-ae. It's Songhua. She was small and seemed so vulnerable. Everyone wanted her, but she came right into my arms. Only for a little while, though. She told me she was twenty, but I think she was lying. I think she must have experienced things most twenty-year-olds don't, so that's probably why she seemed older. She left soon enough." She emptied her glass. A black smudge from her eyelashes shadowed one eye. "She's lucky she was able to cross, but her beauty is actually a burden. Men were drawn to her, and she knew how to sell what she had at the best price. And she came to me, because I had the best, priciest girls in Yanji. She was the most beautiful of all my girls. But if you're that beautiful, you don't have to stay anywhere or listen to anyone."

I stared down at Yong-ae's crumpled face.

Mama glanced at me. "She left about six months ago," she finally said. "Songhua thanked me one day and headed out."

"Where did she go?"

"I didn't ask. She probably went toward more money. Shanghai, probably. That's where money gathers."

"Shanghai," I murmured.

Back at Changbaishan, I got on the computer and looked up Shanghai. The Internet took me to glass-sheathed buildings, the red Oriental Pearl TV Tower, and streets filled with foreigners in crisp white shirts. I searched for her in those pictures.

"We'll be even freer and richer in Shanghai," Dash said excitedly. "Let's go. Let's get rich."

✩ ✩ ✩

Mama introduced us to Old Man Yong-gyu, who was actually only around fifty, a longtime dealer and friend of Zheng Hanmo. He came to Yanji for a couple of weeks each month. We heard that he frequented Beijing and Shanghai, as well as Hong Kong, Singapore, Pyongyang, and Seoul, and that he tipped generously in renminbi, U.S. dollars, Hong Kong dollars, yen, and won. When he met us, he understood immediately that we had fled the North, and perhaps took pity on us; instead of waiters who were better and quicker, he requested us to serve him. He had been the president of Kangdong Group, which distributed North Korean products in northeast China and imported Chinese industrial products for the republic, and he maintained friendly relationships with high-level officials in the Party.

"We're set now," Dash said, grinning. "If Old Man Yong-gyu takes us under his wing, we're safe, even if the SPSD catches up to us."

A month after the introductions, Old Man Yong-gyu called us in. "Would you like some whiskey?"

Dash bowed and took a glass, and Old Man Yong-gyu filled the glass to the brim. Dash turned away politely and downed the entire glass.

"I've been watching you two. You aren't opportunistic like the others. Would you be interested in doing an errand for me? I need two bags delivered to Shanghai."

Dash nodded eagerly.

Old Man Yong-gyu sucked on a cigarette and took an envelope out from his inner jacket pocket. He tossed it on the table. "This should be plenty for travel. You'll receive a generous payment once you deliver the bags. Can you do it?"

Dash kneeled on the floor. "We would be happy to do anything you want," he said solemnly.

"I've already talked to Zheng. Be ready to leave tomorrow morning." Old Man Yong-gyu got up and left.

Bodyguards came in, and one of them placed two booklets on the table. Chinese identification cards. Dash opened them. Our photos were inside. We had taken these pictures a few days ago. I had taken a picture with the two chefs just outside the kitchen and Dash had taken one with the large guard stationed at the entrance and the woman who managed the girls.

"What's your name?" a bodyguard asked.

I looked at my identification card. "Jiang Jiajie," I mumbled.

"Where were you born?"

"Yanji, Jilin Province."

"And you?"

Dash looked down at his card and hesitated. I read his new name for him. "Kai Ludu, born in Changchun, Jilin Province."

On the train the next morning, Dash kept looking at his ID card, grinning. To him, it didn't matter that it was fake. It showed that he was a Chinese citizen, and that was all he cared about. The undulating train screamed along the tracks. Villages, roads, and people gushed past. Dash—no, Kai Ludu— took out his gold-rimmed glasses and put them on. A fraying copy of *Newsweek* was on the luggage rack above. I took it down and began to read a fascinating article.

North Korea's Export of Drugs:
An Underground Economy Encourages Drug Trade
December 16, 2002

Fifty miles from the northern border of China lies Yan-ji, a bustling center for refugees, smugglers, prostitutes, which has become the most important distribution center for North Korean drugs, particularly methamphetamine, in the last fifteen years. Since the collapse of the USSR in 1991, the drug trade at the border between China and North Korea has boomed. The North Korean government has weakened from decreased overseas financial assistance and severe famine that has killed hundreds of thousands of citizens. These difficult circumstances have led to the escape of thousands of North Koreans.

Officials believe that a majority of drugs circulating in China are coming from North Korea. Last year, Chinese border patrol arrested six North Koreans smuggling in illicit substances. According to sources, in North Korea one gram of methamphetamine sells for ten times the price of rice, which goes for $15/kg; in China, the price is even higher, and selling "ice" is often the easiest way to make money. Chinese officials believe that abandoned factories near Hamhung, North Korea, built during Japanese rule, have been churning out methamphetamine continuously.

The drug trade in North Korea dates back to the 1970s with the cultivation of opium. One defector, who escaped from a prison camp, stated that opium was one of the many crops grown by inmates, and that the government allegedly exported the drugs in secret.

Dash looked out the window, cradling his exposed belly. "Gil-mo, I can't believe we're going to Shanghai!"

DAY FOUR: SHANGHAI
February 2003–May 2004

take my old calculator out from under my pillow. Does my math teacher miss this device? I press the numbers gently and see my beloved numbers appear on the screen. Black numbers twinkle against the gray screen. I recall what he told me the last time I saw him. "Gil-mo, the world is a beautiful place."

I hear Angela approaching in 4/4 time. She raps on my cell door. 4/3 time. I don't answer, but she comes in anyway. She rips out the first page in her file and holds it out.

I study it for a long time before turning to her. "Is there only one truth, do you think? Could there be two or more truths?"

She tilts her head. "What do you mean?"

I start drawing on the sheet of paper. "This sequence starts from two. Since it is the first number you add one to get the next number in the sequence. Three is the second number, so you add two to that. And so on until you get this."

"But these aren't all prime numbers."

"I like symmetry, too. And just because I like prime numbers doesn't mean this isn't correct. There's one problem, but there isn't just one answer." I draw three more symbols underneath.

The first sequence is 8, 12, 17, and the one below is 8, 13, 21. They are nearly identical but follow entirely different rules. "The Fibonacci sequence," I explain, "is an infinite sequence that adds the previous number to the number before that. So: 2 / 3 is 0.66666, 3 / 5 is 0.6, 5 / 8 is 0.625, 8 / 13 is 0.615384, 13 / 21 is 0.619047, and so on. The ratio between the two numbers comes closer and closer to the golden ratio of 1:1.618." I think of all the beautiful things that form the golden ratio, from the spiral of a pine cone to the arrangement of petals on a flower to a shell of a nautilus to Leonardo da Vinci's paintings to a sonata to Yong-ae.

Angela stares at my shapes.

"How can you say that the one answer you know is correct when you don't know all the answers?" I ask.

"Well," Angela finally says, "if you know at least one answer that's correct, you know that it's accurate."

"Not knowing everything can be the same as not knowing anything. A little bit of knowledge can be dangerous."

Angela is about to say something else but gives up and sighs. She shakes the sheet of paper she's holding. "Did you read this? Interpol confirmed that you were involved in money laundering in Shanghai. Tell me what happened."

Re: Jiang Jiajie,
Chief Financial Manager of Shanghai Drug Ring
—Shanghai Municipal Bureau of Public Security

From 2003 to 2004, Jiang Jiajie worked as an
accountant for Shanghai-based Kunlun Corporation.
Though his exact date of birth and birthplace are
unknown, Jiang gained the trust of Cheng Xiaogang,
the head of a Shanghai drug ring, and oversaw drug

trade funds and money laundering. In 2004, during the Shanghai Municipal Bureau of Public Security's war on drugs, Kunlun Corporation was disbanded and Cheng was assassinated. Jiang served one year in prison. His whereabouts are unknown upon release.

Shanghai was a whirl of dizzying lights. People walked faster here; I floated along the river of people coursing through the streets, reminded of being tossed in the black Tumen. Where was this colorful cacophony taking me? We made our way to a three story white mansion in a luxurious residential area not far from the river. We gaped up at the house as men in dark suits and sunglasses let us in through the wrought iron gates. A sprinkler misted the manicured lawn dotted with junipers and exotic fruit trees. We stepped into the marble-clad entrance and were shown into the living room.

It smelled like cinnamon. A guard was stationed at the door and another by the window. A man in his forties studied files at a desk in the middle of the room, peering over his gold-rimmed glasses and tapping a calculator. I found myself drawn to the calculator and inched toward the desk. The man was working on a ledger, his eyes shifting from the page to his calculator. I peeked over his shoulder. "Thirty-two thousand eight hundred ninety-seven," I murmured.

His head shot up. He looked back at me then threw a look at one of the guards, who came over and pulled me aside. The man went back to his calculations. Eventually he looked up at me suspiciously. "Hey, you," he hissed. "What did you say?"

"Thirty-two thousand eight hundred ninety-seven."

"How did you know that?"

"That's the sum of all the numbers in the right-hand column," I explained.

"Are you saying that you calculated this whole column in your head, faster than a calculator?"

I shrugged.

A deep voice boomed from near the window, startling us. "Huang, are you done yet?" We hadn't noticed the man, who had been feeding a parrot in a cage hanging by the window.

"Yes, sir," the man said, his demeanor suddenly deferential.

"Bring the books. Don't waste my time."

Huang shoved his ledger in a black leather bag and stood up. "Coming, sir."

Dash and I followed Huang across the living room. The man with the parrot was just over fifty and as large as a bear. Deep wrinkles were set in his narrow forehead, which was topped with thick graying hair, and his nose appeared flat from the excess flesh on his face. He turned toward us.

Dash placed our bags down and wiped the sweat beaded between the folds of his neck. The guards gathered around our bags and emptied them. They cut the bottom of the bags open. To our great surprise, they took out plastic bags filled with white powder. One of them dipped a finger in the powder, tasted it, and nodded.

"Well done," the big man said pleasantly. "Rest up before your journey back."

Dash threw himself on his knees and pulled me down next to him. His thin shirt was plastered on his sweaty back. "We didn't come all the way here to rest, sir," he said urgently. "We have nowhere to go."

"Go back to where you came from," the big man said airily.

"SPSD agents are all over Yanji. They're looking for us."

Dash began to sound desperate. "We'll do anything you want. Please don't send us back."

The parrot squawked. Its owner stroked its yellow feathers. "I suppose I can't send away a bird that flew into my arms on its own," he said, as if to himself, and motioned to one of the guards.

Dash bowed, resting his head on the marble floor. I didn't know what was going on but followed his lead. The floor felt nice and cold; I stayed still for a long time until one of the guards tugged me away.

✪ ✪ ✪

Kunlun was what people called the man with the parrot, after the enormous mountain range spanning 2,500 kilometers with 5,000-meter-tall peaks. Renowned for its extreme arid and cold climate that was harsh on animals and vegetation, the mountain range was the source of both the Yellow River and the Yangtze River as they wound through the entire country. Like his name-sake, Kunlun was enormous. His voice rumbled and his actions were slow but unpredictable. He would be sunny but suddenly cloud over, morphing quickly into a blizzard. People found it difficult to remain near him, so he was often alone.

But Dash and I were different. We could live anywhere as long as there was water and air. We lived behind the mansion, doing any kind of work that was needed. In the early morning, we went shopping for food; we repaired the walls and paved the stone path in the garden; we planted or moved trees; we cleaned the septic tank. Many people ordered us around—the two gardeners, the four cooks, the four housekeepers, the three drivers, and the seven bodyguards. Dash didn't mind; he was just grateful that we had been allowed to stay. "Thousands of farmers from all over the country come here and end up living in the dirtiest, darkest corners," Dash explained to me. "Mr. Kunlun lived in poverty when he was our age. We can be rich like him by the time we're his age." Dash looked off into the distance dreamily.

Hailing from the highlands of Tibet, Kunlun left home with nothing, wandering the border region shared with Myanmar and Thailand. He managed to gild his life by growing poppies in the backwoods, extracting their white powder, and selling it in the cities. $C10H15N$, molecular weight: 149.23 g/mol. Hydrogen in amphetamine was swapped out for the methyl group to make methamphetamine. He arrived in Shanghai at thirty; drugs had brought him immense wealth, allowing him to build a citadel of riches. He bought buildings and people, amassing bodyguards, household staff, lawyers, accountants, the Bureau of Public Security, politicians, businessmen, and prosecutors. At age forty Kunlun was arrested for dealing drugs, but he was freed on bail after his large legal team bribed the judge. He even managed to buy off the prosecutor who had initiated the proceedings against him. Shanghai was his fiefdom.

Dash revered Kunlun. He decided that he would become something more than a mere laborer. He began to transform his flab into hard muscle, working hard at his new project until he was one day allowed to prove his mettle. That sunny day, Dash was working in the garden when a black car screeched to a stop in front of the mansion; two assailants jumped out. Guards managed to chase them from the gates but the assailants were faster. Dash threw down his shears and ran instinctively toward them, but he was no match for professionals. All he could do was stand firm under their blows. Finally, his meaty fist nailed an assailant's chin, giving the guards enough time to catch up and subdue the men. When he caught his breath, he heard applause behind him. The head of security smiled approvingly. "You're as big as an elephant but as fast and strong. It's a waste for you to be a handyman." Dash was immediately reassigned to be a bodyguard, and was issued a black suit and a pair of sunglasses. He was told to move his belongings to the staff rooms on the second floor. Looking worried, Dash asked the head of security if I could share his room, but was shot down.

"But it would be a waste for Gil-mo to be a handyman, too," Dash explained. "He's a math genius. A walking calculator. He's really very talented with numbers."

The head of security pursed his lips and cocked his head. The next day, he brought us to the living room, where we found Kunlun and Huang. My eyes swept over the symmetry of the room—the desk placed squarely in the middle, the curtains tied neatly on either side of the windows, and two juniper trees standing at attention outside, across from each other. Kunlun was winding a large grandfather clock in the corner with a watch key. In Gilmoese, 6:30 was a polite servant, both hands held neatly together. 10:10 signified something to celebrate, open arms cheering happily. I thought about the complicated world behind the face of the clock, the interlocking gears, the tightly wound springs, the motion of a pendulum marking the one second it took to go from one end to the other, driving the two hands. Kunlun closed the glass cover. The pendulum began to swing gently. Tick-tock, tick-tock. Kunlun blocked the sunlight and his graying hair formed ice caps on his head. "The walking calculator, I presume?" he said, turning toward me.

I just liked numbers and calculations; I wasn't a calculator.

"That's him," the head of security answered.

Kunlun looked me over. "Time passes quickly when you're

old," he murmured to himself. "You can see your life rushing past your very eyes by the time you're my age."

I perked up. The relativity of time, my favorite topic. "Time is elastic. Like the phenomenon of time delay," I began. "When you throw a ball inside a moving train, you have to add the speed of the train to the speed of the ball. When the speed of the ball is constant, what would be the speed of the ball in a stopped train?" I went over to the desk and drew a picture on a sheet of paper.

static   in motion

Everyone just stared at me.

"Einstein explained the time delay phenomenon through the theory of relativity," I continued. "Light traveling from a to b looks straight when you're inside the train, but it looks slanted in the direction of the train's movement from outside the train. The premise of the theory of relativity is the principle that the speed of light is always constant. It means that light does not travel 300,000 kilometers a second but that light traveling 300,000 kilometers is one second. Time equals distance divided by speed, but if speed is constant time becomes smaller in proportion to the distance. If you think of the distance ab as 100 and the distance ac as 110, 100 units of time passes in the train while 110 units of time passed outside. The flow of time in a space that moves and a space that is stopped is different and out of sync."

The four looked even more confused.

"As we get older, each day becomes less significant. One day for a ten-day-old baby is 1/10. One day for a one-year-old is 1/365. If the child is born in January or February of a leap year, it's 1/366. For a ten-year-old it's 1/3,652, and for a twenty-year-old it's 1/7,300 plus the number of leap years. For a fifty-year-old it's 1/18,250 plus the number of leap years. The value of a day shrinks in inverse proportion to one's age. So one day is experienced differently depending on how old you are."

Kunlun started laughing. "A walking calculator, indeed. He'll be good to have around."

"I'm not a walking calculator, but I'll be good to have around," I said. "You're kind."

"I've never heard that before." Kunlun grinned. "You can help with the ledgers for the household. That'll free Huang up so he can concentrate on the company's books."

❋ ❋ ❋

The staff rooms were bigger, brighter, and cleaner than the handyman quarters, and they didn't smell like mold or rust. Our room was in perfect symmetry, which pleased me; we had two beds, two small desks, two tables, two lamps, and two picture frames, one side of the room mirroring the other. I continued my handyman tasks while handling the books, buying Kunlun's favorite fruits at the market, changing lightbulbs, and fixing leaky faucets, as well as recommending that we reduce the number of gardeners instead of the cooking staff and installing a computer in the living room. Every morning at six a.m., I took the six papers from the deliveryman and brought them in. I scanned the papers from Shanghai, Beijing, Hong Kong, New York, and Seoul, reading aloud headlines and important articles about politics, major crimes, and the economy as

Kunlun had breakfast. Afterward, I cleaned out the birdcage and replenished the food and water, then cleaned the house. Kunlun taught me how to play go. Though I had hung out with Jae-ha over the go board, I had been more focused on the geometric shapes made by the straight lines of the board and the white and black stones. Kunlun seemed to enjoy the process of instruction more than winning. Every day at four p.m., we stopped what we were doing and played go. A few weeks after my first lesson, I won easily. Kunlun laughed heartily. "I've been playing my whole life, but lost to you!"

✧ ✧ ✧

Every Sunday, the staff took time off in shifts. Dash and I would sleep in, then go to Shanghai Station to watch women getting off the train, looking exhausted. We would walk along the river as the setting sun dyed the water a deep golden hue, and wander down narrow alleys lined with glass doors lit by red bulbs. Women in short *chipao* and thick makeup giggled, grabbing for us. Dash sauntered ahead of me as I shook them off, prompting them to curse at me. I was always looking for Yong-ae, but I was glad that I never spotted her there.

When I had Sunday morning off, I would visit libraries. I would walk among the tall bookshelves, searching for *The Odyssey*. Did Yong-ae ever do what I was doing? Did she end up reading the book? Eventually, I made it through thirty-four library branches. The thirty-fifth was a small library by the Yellow River. I ran my finger along the spines until I got to *The Odyssey*. It was covered in dust. I opened the back cover to check the card. The list started with Jiang Shenzhu on November 21, 1998, and ended with Liu Minglin on June 2, 2003. Fourteen people had checked it out in those five years, and six had borrowed it since 2002. Li Lin, Zhang Ming, Liu Jiawei, Hong Xuancheng, Cao Jialing, and Liu Minglin. I began to read the book idly until I came upon the page where Odysseus returns to Ithaca. I spotted the number written in the margin.

77772

She had been here. Yong-ae had come to this very library and opened this book. Two years ago, I had told her about Kaprekar numbers in front of the rabbit cages. "Somewhere in India, there was a sign that said '3025 km' next to a railroad," I had explained. "One day, Kaprekar, who was a mathematician, saw that the sign had fallen over in a storm and had split into two. It was now 30 and 25. If you add 30 to 25, you get 55, and 55^2 is 3025. So if you split this number in half and add the two parts together and square it, it becomes the number you start with. In Gilmoese, this means that even things that go their separate ways will meet again."

What had Yong-ae said when I told her this story? I couldn't remember. But I recalled what I had told her after explaining Kaprekar's constant—7777 was the square root of the eight-digit Kaprekar number 60481729. I thought of all the Kaprekar numbers.

81: $8 + 1 = 9$, $9^2 = 81$
9801: $98 + 01 = 99$, $99^2 = 9801$
2025: $20 + 25 = 45$, $45^2 = 2025$
3025: $30 + 25 = 55$, $55^2 = 3025$
998001: $998 + 001 = 999$, $999^2 = 998001$

To the right of 7777^2 I wrote 6048 and 1729. I was elated. The formula was now complete. Yong-ae had remembered Gilmoese. This was her way of leaving me a message. She, too, believed that we would meet again. I took the book with me to the front desk and asked for the previous borrowers' contact information, but the librarian told me she couldn't give that out. That was all right, though; she had read this book here, and she still remembered our language. The smell of her hair wound itself around me as I put the book back.

I floated home along the banks of the Yellow River.

"Did something good happen?" Kunlun asked when he saw me. "You look very pleased with yourself."

I didn't answer and went straight up to my room.

PALE DAYTIME MOON

Kunlun owned three cars with three-liter engines—a Mercedes-Benz, a Lexus, and a Hyundai Equus—and his three drivers were on call around the clock, playing mahjongg as they waited by the garage. Kunlun often preferred to walk to his appointments, and when he did I went along. The July sun blasted the sidewalk and hot air snaked up my legs. I made up games with numbers I encountered in the street, picking them out from signs and license plates and even branching into addresses and the number of floors in a building. I thought of the street with an empty lot next to three-, one-, and four-story buildings as Pi Street. Prime Number Street was the busy thoroughfare lined with eleven-, thirteen-, seventeen-, and nineteen-story buildings. Luxury cars, buses, taxis, and bicycles rolled past in a jumble. I preferred the cars with the older license plates, composed solely of numbers without any Latin letters. I caught the lucky license plate number 88888—with 8 pronounced *ba*, similar to *fa* in *fa chai*, meaning to earn wealth, that must have been unimaginably expensive to obtain. With 9 signifying plenty and 7 resembling the word for happiness, both of those numbers would have also been at a premium.

Kunlun purchased a fine suit at a department store and sticky cockroach traps at a rundown marketplace. We bought a few other things. I counted out the bills and he put the receipts in his pocket.

"Would you like something cold to drink?" Kunlun asked as he strode ahead.

"Coca-Cola, please."

He got himself a green tea and handed me a can of Coke. With a hiss, the gas escaped. My tongue prickled, and I felt rich. It reminded me of Jae-ha.

Back home, I put the food in the refrigerator and placed the new pruning shears in the shed. I planted the new flower seeds in the garden and watered them, and changed the rubber ring in a leaky faucet. Kunlun unfolded the receipts and recorded them in his ledger, using a large calculator. "Double check that everything's accurate, Gil-mo."

I took a look at savory 5s, warm 8s, and mushroomy 3s. Nine had the funk of long-fermented food, and 7 crunched and shattered. "The calculations are correct but the sum is wrong."

Kunlun peered at his ledger.

"The fedora was twenty percent off," I reminded him. "It was marked as 2,300 yuan, but we only paid 1,840 yuan. But the full price is on the receipt. You forgot to tally our drinks, since we didn't get a receipt. One cup of green tea is 2 yuan and the Coke was 4 yuan. So you have to subtract 460 yuan and add 6 yuan. The sum should be 4,396 yuan." I dumped the coins out of his wallet and counted the bills. "Since you have 1,787 yuan in your wallet, that checks out. You initially had 6,183 yuan."

Beginning the next day, Kunlun allowed me to reconcile the receipts.

✬ ✬ ✬

Dash and I began accompanying Kunlun on a special outing each Wednesday and Friday. Dash sat next to the driver and I was in the back with Kunlun. The Mercedes drove into an exclusive residential area in Gubei. Kids giggled on swings; balls bounced merrily on expansive tennis courts; large, well-groomed dogs barked under verandas; and a yellow school bus let out an orderly line of schoolchildren. We drove up to a gated community with a sign that said EASTERN MANHATTAN. The CCTV over the gate blinked, reading our license plate, and we were let in. The car glided along the hedge-lined driveway and stopped at an opulent Victorian-style four-story building, which had two entrances. Large terraces flanked either side of the entrances. Dash lumbered out and opened the door for Kunlun, who got out and smoothed his clothes, and they went into the entrance to the right.

The driver loosened his bowtie and leaned his seat back. "We're free to do whatever until he comes back out."

I sat still in the backseat. I didn't pay attention to the loud whine of cicadas or squint against the bright sunlight.

The driver poked his head out of the window and looked up. "Do you know how expensive that place is?" he asked conspiratorially. "I went in once to do an errand. It's like an emperor lives there! The floor is made of shiny black marble. Even the walls are marble, but they're brown. We'll never be able to afford a place like that, even if we work our entire lives."

I looked up, too. "So a really rich person lives here, then?"

"Well, if you're really pretty, you can live in a place like this." He turned to grin at me. "An old rich man and a poor beautiful girl have a lot of things the other person wants."

"Like what?"

The driver shook his head. "Money and time, of course. The old man buys time and the pretty girl makes money. You know. The oldest deal in the history of the world."

I didn't understand. How could you buy time, and how could you make money with your looks?

"He bought this place about half a year ago. That was surprising on its own. But the stuff he got his new lady! He got her a car and a maid, too. He really fell for this girl."

Just then, Dash came out of the entrance, Kunlun following him. The driver quickly cinched his bowtie and pulled his seat up. Dash and Kunlun waddled up and got in the car.

"Let's go," Kunlun said.

I looked out at the gardeners wearing wide-brimmed straw hats. Suddenly, the glass door on the fourth floor terrace slid open and a girl ran out in a white polka-dot dress. The breeze moved her wavy, shoulder-length hair, revealing her pale, moon-like forehead. The hem of her dress puffed up like a sail. She was smiling and waving. I waved back without realizing what I was doing. I kept waving even as the car turned at the juniper hedge and drove toward the gates.

✪ ✪ ✪

Two weeks later, Kunlun handed me a black cast-iron key as I changed the parrot's water. "This is the key to the safe. That's where all the ledgers are. You take over the accounting, all right?"

In the safe, I found seven ledgers; separate ones for his trips, for hospitality, for staff salaries, for additional security, for the cars, and a couple others. Kunlun settled me at a desk at the entrance to the office. I organized receipts and bills and recorded expenses and income. After a few weeks, I was able to anticipate how much money went in and out each day, taking into consideration rent from twelve tenants, electric and water bills, and staff salaries. A few weeks after that, I was able to calculate change in income and expenses by month and by year for the previous three years, and drew a graph denoting the changes. Pleased with my work, Kunlun handed over several additional ledgers. "Don't pay attention to the items. Just see if the numbers are correct."

I went over each book carefully over two hours. My head, lips, and pen moved quickly in sync. Finally, I looked up. "The calculations are correct," I announced.

Kunlun nodded in satisfaction. "Good. So nothing's wrong with them."

"I didn't say there was nothing wrong with them."

Kunlun frowned. "What do you mean? You just said the calculations are correct."

"These numbers don't fit with Benford's Law."

Kunlun looked exasperated.

I tried again. "Thieves always leave clues behind." I grabbed the day's *Huanqiu Shibao*, *Wall Street Journal*, and *Chosun Ilbo*. "Could you please count how many of each leading digit appears in the papers?"

"I don't have to count," Kunlun said, growing annoyed. "All numbers appear at random. I suppose the probability of any one number appearing is one out of ten."

I just stared at him until he finally picked up the papers and tallied the numbers. He showed me what he had scrawled on a piece of paper, humoring me.

1: 30%, 2: 18%, 4: 10%, 5: 8%, 6: 7%, 7: 6%, 8: 5%, 9: 4%.

He frowned. "There are too many 1s and too few 9s. How can different papers from different countries have such consistent results?"

"Because of Benford's Law," I explained. "An overwhelming portion of numbers begin with 1. The bigger the number, the less frequently it appears. A number that begins with 9, for example, is less than 5 percent."

Kunlun looked confused.

"Benford was an engineer at General Electric. In 1938, he was looking at the census when he realized that there were more numbers starting with 1 than any other. He discovered that this was the case for almost any statistic, like stock prices, lengths of rivers, batting and earned run averages, populations, and so forth."

Kunlun narrowed his eyes.

"Let's say you decide to give a bodyguard a bonus at random," I said, trying a different tack. "Five guards draw straws, and the probability of someone picking 1 is one out of five, so 20 percent. The more guards there are, the probability of someone picking one decreases. So if you have nine guards, the probability is 1 / 9, so 11 percent. But if you have 10 guards, the probability of drawing a number beginning with a 1, 1 or 10, becomes 2/10, so 20 percent. With 11, 12, 13, or 14 people, the probability keeps increasing. By the time you have 19 people, you have 11 in 19 odds of drawing a number with a 1 in it. But with 20 or 30 people, the probability goes back down. When you're at 99, it's 11/99, which is 11 percent. When you hit 100, the probability of drawing a number with a 1 in it increases until 199." I drew a graph on the paper.

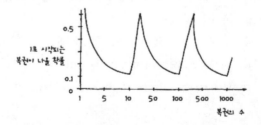

"The y axis is the probability of picking a number starting with 1 and the x axis is the number of straws. The probability vacillates between 58 percent and 11 percent. According to Benford's Law, the universal probability of a number's first digit, *n*, is log (*n* + 1) − log *n*. If *n* is 1, log 2 − log 1 = 0.301, thus 30.1 percent."

Kunlun grimaced. "What are you talking about? What does this have to do with the ledgers?"

"The ledgers contain a random sample of unspecified numbers. So it has to have more numbers that start with 1 than with bigger numbers. If not, something is wrong."

"What do you mean?"

"Either the calculations are wrong, or the ledgers were manipulated."

Kunlun began shaking his head slowly.

"There were some minor differences in all the ledgers, but, overall, numbers starting with 1 didn't show up as much as they should have, and numbers starting with 5 or 6 appeared too frequently."

Kunlun gritted his teeth, though his face remained placid. He summoned the head of security and whispered to him, which sent him rushing out of the room.

✪ ✪ ✪

A few days later, Huang stopped coming by. A week later, I opened the *Huanqiu Shibao* at the breakfast table and froze. His smiling face was emblazoned in the paper, next to a picture of a Mercedes with a crumpled hood being hauled out of the river.

"Anything interesting today?" Kunlun asked.

"'Chairman of Goldman Corporation Dies in Car Accident'," I read out. I looked at Kunlun, who nodded for me to go on. "'Goldman Corporation chairman Huang Taimin died last night in a car crash on Renmin Avenue at 1 a.m. Eyewitnesses stated that Huang had tried to avoid a car that crossed the center divider before crashing through the guardrail into the Yellow River. His sudden death marks a big loss to the Shanghai business sector, as Goldman Corporation handles accounting and consulting for many local businesses and foreign investment firms. Huang has led several large-scale mergers and acquisitions, including a takeover of Indonesia's Mandarin Resort Hotel on behalf of Kunlun Corporation four years ago. The funeral will be held on the morning of the 16th.'"

Kunlun cracked a small smile. "Hmm."

I put the *Huanqiu Shibao* down and opened the *Wall Street Journal.*

"We should send flowers to the funeral," he told me. "Now that Huang's dead, you're in charge of reconciling all the books."

THE CORD THAT HAS LEFT ONE POINT ON EARTH

In March 2002, Tiancheng Corporation moved its headquarters from Sichuan to Shanghai. Though ostensibly a construction company, its main business was investing in bars and the drug trade; a showdown with Kunlun was inevitable. Tiancheng recruited away Kunlun's executives and did everything possible to take over his customers and accounts, but Kunlun remained strong. Around the end of November, Tiancheng changed its tactics.

Dash and I were accompanying Kunlun in his Mercedes one day when a large dump truck sped toward us. Though the driver braked and turned the wheel, the hood of the Mercedes was crumpled and the windshield was shattered. The driver broke his left shoulder; Kunlun emerged with a scratch on his forehead, and Dash and I weren't injured. The truck driver was unscathed. The official investigation concluded that the truck's brakes were faulty, but Kunlun's security team discovered that the truck driver used to work at a Sichuan construction site. Everyone was on edge. The head of security doubled the number of guards patrolling the perimeter of the mansion and made sure that Kunlun was never alone. It became increasingly difficult for Kunlun to leave the house, so I became his proxy.

"Deliver this to Eastern Manhattan," Kunlun said, handing me a thick envelope containing the girl's monthly allowance. I got in the Lexus idling in the garage and the driver took a bumpy but safe shortcut. Fifteen minutes later, we were at Eastern Manhattan. The sprinklers misted everything, including the car. We pulled up to the entrance of the villa, and I checked to make sure that the envelope was still in my pocket.

Bodyguards were stationed at the stairs and in the hallway of the fourth floor. They nodded at me. One pressed the doorbell, two short bursts, one long, one short, then a final very long one. I heard slippers coming up to the door. The lock turned.

Inside, I handed over the envelope without making eye contact. A servant placed a large glass of Coca-Cola on a table beside me. Tight bubbles popped the surface and bounced onto the table. Light foam brewed quietly in my mouth and exploded, tickling my nose, and eventually turned into a fragrant burp. White frost on the glass condensed into droplets and trickled down the sides.

"You still like Coke, I see."

I realized I knew this voice. I sneaked a quick glance at her thick, shiny hair, her animated brows, and her plump lips. Her cheeks had filled out and her curves had become even more attractive. Her full bosom made her look haughty. I recognized the golden ratio in her part and throughout her face—red lipstick, black mascara, and hair dye couldn't mask those.

"You haven't changed one bit," she said, amused.

"Your face still has all the beautiful ratios," I managed.

Yong-ae's voice turned chilly. "I'm not the same, though. I'm Cao Jialing from Hunan, now."

"You're still the same," I said. "I'm Jiang Jiajie, but that's just a name. I've seen your new name before."

"How?"

"Who else would have written the Kaprekar number in *The Odyssey* in the library by the Yellow River?"

She frowned. She reached over and took my glass and gulped the rest of my drink. "So you've been searching for me all this time?"

Her voice sounded annoyed. Was it wrong for me to look for her? I must have looked puzzled.

"Don't be stupid," she snapped. "We were friends once, sure. But now our lives are headed in different directions. I'm free and wealthy now, and I'm going to do whatever it takes to maintain that."

"I'll do the same, then," I said. "I'll be freer and wealthier, too."

Yong-ae narrowed her eyes. "That doesn't suit you. You're too good. I'm not. Don't waste your time wandering around libraries. Don't bother coming after me, okay?"

I was confused. "Are you saying there was a better way to find you?"

She laughed. "It's no coincidence that I came to Shanghai and met Kunlun, you realize. It isn't a coincidence that we're face-to-face right now."

"Exactly!" I cried. She understood my theory so well. "You're holding one end of the cord that is staked at Muryong Prison Camp. I was holding the other end. We were bound to meet again."

She snorted. "No, that's not what I mean." She looked at me pityingly. "Gil-mo, I came here the same way you did. I delivered a bag for Old Man Yong-gyu."

My eyes widened.

"It wasn't just us, either," Yong-ae said, looking exasperated. "Being a drug mule is the easiest way for people like us to make something of ourselves. Do you understand? We delivered bags to the same place, following the same route. If you understood that, you wouldn't have had to waste so much time. You could have easily found me."

I nodded. I didn't ask her any details, like how she crossed the Tumen, how many men she had to know to get here safely, how she had become Kunlun's lady. I didn't know if she was happy or if she ever thought of me. I didn't really want to know; I knew people had to do things to survive. I remembered how mothers sold daughters for a few yuan in Yanji, how the SPSD dragged young men back to the republic, and how men roamed around trying to find defectors to make a few quick bucks.

Yong-ae finally cracked a smile. "Kunlun saved me," she said in a low voice. "He insists that I'm the one who saved him, though. I guess we saved each other."

"But this isn't your life," I said, suddenly impassioned. "You're not a bird in a fancy cage."

"There's nowhere for me to go," Yong-ae said gently. "Even if there were, I can't leave him. Not now."

I cocked my head. "Why not?"

"He needs me. And he was there for me when I was roaming the streets, drunk."

I looked out at the terrace. The sun was setting. The Lexus was waiting for me outside. That night, I returned to our room and found Dash watching a movie. Chow Yun-fat was in a gun battle with the bad guys, twelve against—well, 0.7, because Chow was shot in the leg and was dying. Dash was engrossed in his movie, tossing snacks in his half-open mouth.

"I saw Yong-ae."

Dash didn't pay me any attention.

"I saw Yong-ae," I said, a little louder.

Dash sprang up from his bed. He pulled out all the details before grabbing his head in dismay. "Are you telling me that the girl you're looking for is the lady at the Manhattan?" he whispered fearfully. "Gil-mo, don't you ever tell Kunlun!"

"Why not?" I had told Kunlun about Yong-ae before. Kunlun was rooting for me to find her.

"He doesn't know that Yong-ae is his girl."

"So?"

"What do you mean, 'so'?" Dash stared daggers at me. "He'll kill you, and nobody will ever find out."

"I can't lie to him."

"You're not lying. You're just not telling him everything you know. It's a secret, right? A secret between us. So it's not really a lie. All you have to do is keep our secret."

"Okay."

Dash let out a sigh. He resumed his snacking and turned back to his movie. "I want to be just like Chow Yun-fat. That's how I want to go when I die. So cool."

"Dying by gunfire is cool?" Sometimes Dash made no sense.

"It's cool to die as you're fighting the bad guys," he clarified, guzzling his Coke.

RIDING THE SILVER BACK OF TIME

"'State Administration of Taxation Investigates Shanghai Real Estate Firm'," I read to Kunlun, who was listening peacefully with his eyes closed. "'Upon its months-long investigation of real estate group Kunlun Corporation, the Shanghai Municipal Bureau of Local Taxation has concluded that the corporation has evaded paying 60 million yuan in taxes. The Shanghai Municipal Bureau of Public Security descended on Kunlun hotel, arresting twenty-three servers who brokered prostitution and collecting evidence that Cheng Xiaogang, the head of the organization, known as Kunlun, received illegal revenue through embezzlement and manipulation of stock prices. Cheng grew up penniless before going on to build the major corporation, and has refused all media requests, shrouding his life in secrecy. In 1980, he was investigated for drug distribution, but by the end of the 1980s, he had earned 20 million yuan by manufacturing counterfeit high-end liquor. He has since expanded his business by establishing a real estate development company widely understood to be a front for illicit operations, including unlawful evictions, and has become one of the richest men in Shanghai. Six years ago, he embarked on corporate takeover of hotels and resorts in Shanghai and Hong Kong, continuing to amass wealth through prostitution, gambling, and loan shark activities. Cheng has allegedly paid a 300,000-yuan bribe to Feng Jianhou, the former head of the

Shanghai Municipal Bureau of Public Security, and bought off high-level government officials and the National People's Congress. Last October, Shanghai Party Secretary Jian Zhenxi launched a war on crime, and as a result the Bureau of Public Security detected Kunlun Corporation's illegal acts. However, Cheng has mistakenly relied on his influence, leading to the shutdown of the corporation and Kunlun Hotel, the arrest of Feng, and the downfall of Chen's protectors.'"

Every time I uttered his name, Kunlun's thick gray eyebrows trembled. The two-year battle with Tiancheng Corporation over Shanghai had drained him. In his fight, he had paid for a lot, including much of his wealth. In the last several months, he had become an old man.

Tiancheng's attacks had persisted from all directions. They used anything they could to constrict his influence; they weren't afraid of using violence or informants, conspiracies, and betrayals. Kunlun's bodyguards were shot and stabbed or found themselves in car accident after car accident. Hong Chaohong, Tiancheng's CEO, doubled the bribes that officials who had watched out for Kunlun were receiving. Officials who refused bribes were arrested under suspicion of bribery. Kunlun's every move was under scrutiny; city health inspectors came to his hotel every day, and the safety department's inspector basically lived at his construction sites. The tax bureau combed through the books of Kunlun Corporation and its subsidiaries. Kunlun's people betrayed him or were arrested, and staff at his mansion dwindled. Without a caretaker, grass overtook the garden; without cooks, meals became bland. Cars stood in the garage, covered in dust. Only a few of us remained.

Kunlun turned to feed his parrot. "The Bureau of Public Security suggested a compromise," he said heavily. "If I leave the city, I won't be arrested. Tiancheng is targeting my assets and territory, not my life. If I'm lucky, I'll be able to take enough cash to live out the rest of my life."

"Where would you go?" Dash asked. As Kunlun's fortunes crumbled, Dash's girth had begun to deflate; as he began to lose weight, he grew nervous, believing that freedom and wealth were abandoning him.

"They're telling me I should go to Macau within the next three months," Kunlun said. He sighed. "They want to keep me locked up on that small island."

The turf war had effectively ended. Kunlun went to the Bureau of Public Security to negotiate a dignified retreat. He advised us to leave him and find our own way, but he was all we knew; after all, we were his cooks, bodyguards, handymen, and drivers. Kunlun got us all Macauan passports and went to the banks to wire his remaining money to an account on the island.

Two weeks later, Dash went to Pudong Station to buy four tickets to Zhuhai. Kunlun and Dash were to ride in car number 9, while Yong-ae and I were to be in the next car; half of us would escape, no matter what happened to the others. When Dash returned home with the tickets, Kunlun put one in a manila envelope and handed it to me. "Deliver this to Manhattan," he told me. "Tell her to come to Pudong Station at noon tomorrow. She should take her seat. Tell her to bring as little luggage as possible."

That night, I packed my things in my worn knapsack. I added three triangles, Captain Miecher's notebook, my calculator, a few newspaper articles, and my new passport. I curled up in bed. Dash tossed and turned, the springs in his bed squeaking each time he moved.

"I hope Macau will be great," Dash said hopefully. "We probably can't even imagine what it's going to be like, just like we had no idea what Shanghai would be like when we were in Yanji." His words twinkled in the dark.

At the train station the next day, Kunlun wiped his sweaty arms with a handkerchief and looked up at the red clock tower. It was 11:57. The sunlight bleached the square. I placed my hands over my ears and squinted. Dash led the way, elbowing people aside. We crossed the crowded square and entered the station. Cold sweat beaded my forehead. Dash walked ahead and Kunlun pulled me along by my sleeve. The speakers blared. "Train 352 departing at 12:12 boarding on platform eight." We took a flight of stairs down to the platform. Dash was on edge. Kunlun, too, was nervous, looking all around him. We passed cars 3, 4, and 5. The ticket in my hand was damp with sweat. The booming speakers made me dizzy. The hot air from the train hurt my head. We were at car 8. Yong-ae was inside, looking anxious. Dash and Kunlun walked a few steps ahead of me, toward the next car. I wasn't sure if they had seen her. She gave me a tiny smile, then her eyes grew wide. She froze. I tore my eyes away from her.

Four men had descended on Dash; both his arms were twisted behind him; he was on the ground. They were kicking him. He hunched over, his mouth filling with blood. "Gil-mo, take him and run!" he croaked. Kunlun had taken a few steps backward. Two more men came up to him and one took something from his jacket. He hugged Kunlun, then let go quickly. They quickly disappeared the way we had come. Kunlun crumpled, then straightened and looked into the train. Yong-ae was leaning on the window, tears streaking mascara down her face. Dash limped over and kneeled on the platform to pull Kunlun up. Blood trickled out through Kunlun's hands, which were clutching his stomach. People gathered around us. Someone was shouting. Three officers ran over. Kunlun lay back and gazed at me gently. His eyes closed slowly. Two officers grabbed our arms behind our backs and cuffed us, and the third felt for Kunlun's pulse. He shook his head. They loaded him onto a white stretcher.

"Don't look at her," Dash whispered to me. "Remember, we don't know her."

The train began to move as the officers pushed us toward the entrance to the station. She passed us, her eyes dazed, her face streaked in black. We hadn't made it. One died, two were arrested, and only one was able to leave. The cuffs dug into my wrists.

Dear Yong-ae,

As you probably guessed, I was arrested the moment you left Shanghai. The Shanghai Municipal Bureau of Public Security put us on trial, and we got one-year sentences. The brick walls here are tall and covered in moss. Sometimes we can't tell what the weather is like outside. We can't tell if time is passing. We wear wide blue pants that are worn at the knees, and we live with six other men in a small cell with a heavy steel door. We have eight spoons and a hole in the ground for a toilet. We eat three meals a day, circle the yard, watch TV, then go to sleep.

Dash has lost a lot of weight since we got here. Five kilos a month. He gets heavier the happier he is, and he gets happier the heavier he gets. I think he's depressed. He doesn't snore anymore; his neck lacks folds now and his chin is sharp. His bones stick out of his back. Sometimes, when he's sleeping, he smiles. Maybe he's smiling to say I shouldn't worry, that we will leave soon. When we leave, he'll be happy again and start gaining weight.

I couldn't do anything when Kunlun died. I clasped

my hands together behind my back and prayed. I hope he found his way to heaven.

Did you arrive safely in Macau? I'll find you again, wherever you are. When we get out, we'll come to Macau, where we were all supposed to go.

Gil-mo

DAY FIVE: MACAU
June 2005—February 2006

Re: Jiang Jiajie, Suspected of Fraudulent Gambling
and Murder at Macau's Tomorrow Casino
—Public Security Police Force of Macau

Under the pseudonym Wei Zhenmin, Jiang Jiajie devel-
oped a fraudulent gambling technique that he deployed
in the three leading casinos in Macau and was barred
from entry. In December 2005, he won several hundred
thousand dollars on roulette, and two months later
he won $800,000 at a high-stakes illegal casino in a
game that involved Saudi and Singaporean nationals.
That same day, he participated in a shootout between
illegal gambling rings by the coast, which produced 11
casualties, and disappeared. He is wanted by Interpol
for first-degree murder.

Rock, paper, scissors—three variables with unique values, probability, and relativity. Scissors cut paper but are crushed by rock, while paper wraps and vanquishes rock. I like to greet people with that game; nobody is unhappy even when he loses, and everyone is happy when he wins.

"Rock, paper," I call out.

Angela sticks out her fist. My palm is out. We play two more times; three wins out of three for me! I win frequently. She seems to suspect that I'm cheating.

"Mitsui Yoshizawa was a professor at Tokyo University of Science. He conducted an experiment of 11,567 rock-paper-scissors games. Rock came out 35 percent of the time, while paper was 33.3 percent and scissors was 31.7 percent. I once played 1,428 games in a row and got similar results. Theoretically, it's a fair game, but when you opt for paper first, you have a higher likelihood of winning."

"What if it's a draw?"

"The probability that your opponent will choose the same one is 22.8 percent. So let's say you draw with rock. If you go with scissors next, you won't lose, since the other person will go with scissors or paper. See, it's a very simple game theory." When I learned about game theory in math class, I was awed by its complicated clarity. It was applied to submarine battles in World War II, and it's equally applicable to economics, business, politics, and psychology. After all, they're all battles. It's just a matter of one against one, one against many, or one against everyone. Everything in life is a game. The housewife walking into a market embarks on intense haggling, the student in a classroom grapples with grades, lovers play coy games to be more adored, a boss and employee negotiate salary, and politicians tussle with the opposing party.

Angela nods, understanding where I'm going with this. "War and hostile takeovers use noncooperative game theory. It's just like the prisoner's dilemma—if two prisoners are being interrogated separately and both deny their crime, each receives one year. If they both confess, they each get two. The problem is when only one person confesses; that one will be set free, but the other will be given three years. So what would the two choose?"

I get excited. "If they both deny it to the end, they each get one year. So that's two years total. If one person denies it and one person confesses, that's three total. If they both confess, they get four total. So what benefits the individual doesn't benefit the whole."

It's just like the roulette wheel; it spins, and the game continues. Banks deals me something new each time he comes into my cell—evidence that I'm a murderer, a gambler, a fugitive. How do I show them that their evidence is wrong? I have to go back to the roulette wheel that will determine my fate.

HOW TO WIN AGAINST FATE

On April 26, 2005, Dash and I stepped out the prison gates. We left Shanghai and moved south, through cities and towns linked by the road. Sometimes we walked or ran, and other times we hitchhiked, stole bicycles, perched on top of a mound of fertilizer on the back of one truck, and hid between planks of lumber in another. Dash began to gain his heft back as he began to feel freer and happier. We picked up odd jobs at each stop, working on a farm, as porters in a store, as street cleaners. Dash usually did a larger part of my job as well as his own. Roads barreled toward us and passed us by. We picked our way through alleys covered in filth, walked down streets under faintly glimmering stars, and trudged along unpaved roads blooming with dust. I grew taller and Dash grew fatter.

In Zhuhai we hit several of the biggest bars in town. In one bar, a man sidled up to Dash and asked if he would like to gamble in Macau. Dash's girth and his gold-rimmed glasses must have made him look wealthy. The man told us about beautiful girls who would stay with us and look after our every need. "There's nothing quite like gambling and girls," he said, "and it's best to enjoy them at the same time." He tapped cigarette ash on the floor, blowing out a cloudy stream of smoke.

I took out Yong-ae's photograph from my pocket.

He took a good look and grimaced. "That bitch! You know where she is?"

I shook my head.

He downed a glass of whiskey. "She told me she needed work," he complained. "Her Chinese wasn't great, but what a face! I liked her tenacity. Very northeast. I even gave her an advance and had her accompany a VIP client to Macau. She could have changed her life. But she ran off when she got there."

The man couldn't know that Yong-ae didn't want to change her life; all she wanted was to get to Macau. The next morning, we packed our bags, having promised the man we would call him once we found her. Forty-seven days after leaving prison, we arrived in Macau.

✪ ✪ ✪

"Attention, please," called Dash at the entrance of Megasquare Casino. "Knives, guns, and other weapons are prohibited. No pictures!" Now known as Hu Enlai, he was an hourly security guard at the casino. His neck had regained its fleshy contours, and his hair was shiny with product.

Customers looked around in amazement when they stepped foot on the 12,891-square-meter floor, where five hundred slot machines clattered and dumped chips with great fanfare. People surrounded dealers at tables on one side. Megasquare wasn't as big as the Wynn Macau or the Venetian Macao, but it was a popular destination for serious gamblers as it drew fewer casual tourists. I enjoyed being a janitor, wearing a mask and rubber gloves as I mopped the hallway and wiped down machines, turning everything orderly and clean. People tended to be drawn to certain machines; those next to a pillar or near the hallway or in the corner were never as popular. I noticed that people avoided machines if they witnessed someone winning at them, probably believing that a jackpot wouldn't hit the same machine twice, although the likelihood of hitting a jackpot on a given machine had nothing to do with what had happened in the past.

I discovered something interesting a few weeks into my observations. When I wiped down an unpopular machine with a new detergent, more people sat in front of it, staying 14 percent longer and increasing their bets by 23 percent. But two days later, the traffic to the machine would go down to normal. After experimenting with a few different possibilities, I came to the conclusion that the scent of the new detergent was attracting customers. Dash relayed my discovery to the floor manager, who looked doubtful. I unspooled the data I had gathered, analyzing the location and manufacture date of the lowest occupancy machines, jackpot frequency, the number of guests sitting at the machines with the highest occupancy rate, average occupancy rate, guest flow, and locations of unpopular machines. I explained how the occupancy rates changed according to my cleaning schedule.

Dash drove home the point. "If we can control how the machines smell at any given time, we'll get even greater results."

The manager's eyes glinted.

Dash hesitated. "Or—does this not make sense?"

"I don't care if it does," the manager replied. "As long as the guests sit there longer and bet more."

I was given ownership of the scent project, identifying scents that worked in certain locations and in specific weather. Instead of mopping, I got to check the machines and spray them with scent. I wandered the aisles of slot machines with a spritzer and a dry rag, calculating coincidences and the house edge of each individual machine, which was the sum of the prize money multiplied by the probability of the win. I calculated that the machines with three slots and twenty symbols gave us a house edge of

200 × 3 / 20. If you added each of the house edges of all of the machines derived from this formula, I could get the house edge for the entire casino. I assigned each machine its unique number and collected jackpot dates, daily average number of customers, occupation time, and average bets. Depending on the machine's conditions, I sprayed it with the appropriate scent, allowing each machine to play to its best abilities. I stood back and watched guests rush toward the machines.

✩ ✩ ✩

Machine 2-57 hit a jackpot. Three men had become penniless at that very machine. A young man with dried blood crusted under his nose had dozed at it, his hand gripping the lever, and a Japanese woman won $3,000 on her first-ever visit to a casino. Slot machines weren't fair, not really. A guest at a machine wasn't just playing against his machine; he was facing off against all the machines on the floor. If five hundred machines had a win rate of 94.7 percent, the casino earned 5.3 percent. Clear-headed adventurers preferred blackjack, which allowed for prediction, and competitive risk-takers were drawn to baccarat, putting everything on chance.

Victims abounded from this rigged game. In the back alleys of the spectacular casinos wandered former guests, chased away by guards and brutalized by gangs. Having squandered everything for the promise of a quick buck, they exchanged money for foreigners, hired by casinos to lure customers in. They believed that casinos were their only chance to take back all they had lost. That was where we met Oh Hyeon-su, a businessman who had come from Seoul three years ago but was unable to return home. In the casinos, he had lost several million, some of which he had taken from his company, now defunct. He lived in a run-down place, earning $100 a day from odd jobs, obstinately wearing his old suit. He always showed up at a casino with a black briefcase, changing $5,000 chips at the cage. His goal was to win $100 a day, but mainly it was not to lose; no matter how well he was playing, he got up as soon as he was down $100. His win rate was fairly high. He sent his earnings to his college-student son in Seoul.

Mr. Oh took to us and liked giving advice. "You have to wear a suit in a casino. Otherwise they'll look down on you."

"But it's because you don't have any other clothes, right?" I asked.

He laughed and smoothed his gray hair away from his face.

"What's the best way to win against the house?" asked Dash.

Mr. Oh looked toward the strait, breathing in salty air. "You don't. You can't."

"Even if you win a little every day?"

"Nobody wins against the house."

"So are you just lucky, or are you really good?"

"That's making pocket money," Mr. Oh explained. "That isn't winning. You're just getting ready to lose big. You're caught on a line and dragged around."

Dash let out a long plume of smoke toward the ocean. He glanced at me. "Do you think that's right? Is there no way to win against the house?"

"I'll need to calculate that," I told him.

THE PLACE WHERE SHE LIVES

On my days off I roamed around the strait and islands, staring at the waves, and sat in hotel lobbies, watching people coming and going. At night, I walked down dark streets back home to our small one-room place. She had to be here somewhere. Somewhere in these 29.5 square kilometers that included the Macau peninsula and the islands of Taipa and Coloane. Could we have brushed past each other in a busy street one glittering night?

One Sunday in August, I finally saw her. She was standing in the hallway of the Prima Hotel, in front of the ballroom, smiling broadly. I ran up to her and stared, almost nose to nose. She was inside a frame, 60 centimeters by 1 meter, almost the golden ratio. Her hair, dyed light brown, grazed her shoulders, and her long eyelashes and smoky eye shadow floated in the darkness. She looked older. Her low-cut dress sparkled. It reminded me of the wings of a dragonfly. Under her photo was the following, in both Chinese and English:

10:00–10:30 p.m.
Sarah Kang 撒拉 姜

She wasn't Yong-ae or Songhua or even Jialing; she was now a singer in a hotel club. Just as I was no longer Gil-mo but Jiajie, and Dash had become Enlai. I crouched in the hallway, watching the second hand of a grandfather clock ticking in a circle.

The past rushed over me—the rutted, dust-covered roads; rivers sunken in darkness; sparkling tears of the imprisoned and chased; the rotting eaves that sheltered us from rain; puddles on the ground; dry lips and eyelids crusted with sleep; death spreading across fields. I stared at her, thinking that beauty wasn't only what was new and pretty but also made of old, vanishing parts. Without the passage of time, nothing would be beautiful. I watched Yong-ae's photograph as I waited for ten p.m. to roll around. Soon, I heard singing. I followed the sound.

After her performance, she spotted me. "You look good," she called, waving, pushing away the time we had been apart. Nothing in her face hinted at what had happened—not Kun-lun's death, nor my and Dash's imprisonment, nor her journey here.

I raised my hand in greeting. "You look like you put on a bit of weight."

She laughed, a hand on her sparkling black waist. "I suppose I changed a bit. People call me Sarah." She led me by the sleeve to the elevator.

Blood rushed to my ears until they popped as we hurtled upward. The number 28 lit up and the doors opened to a lounge. We settled by the window overlooking the dark strait. She crossed her legs, the hem of her ankle-length dress winding around her feet.

"I couldn't find any work when I got here," Yong-ae said. "So I walked around the port, singing to myself. That drew gamblers and tourists, and a few dropped coins in front of me. Someone mentioned that I should audition for the club here, and here I am."

Her stage makeup made her look like a different person. Neon lights flared from the top of the building across the way, turning her face red periodically. Yong-ae took out a crumpled pack of cigarettes from her bra and lit one. She inhaled. A waiter brought her a whiskey on the rocks.

"You've become a true capitalist," I commented.

She shrugged. "It's just what it is here. Someone giving you a helping hand turns out to be the devil. Money slips through your fingers like water. Darkness overtakes the lights of the casinos, and the rich become poor." She took a sip.

"But we did find freedom," I countered.

"I didn't leave to find freedom," she scoffed. "I never knew what that was, so I didn't even know it was something I wanted."

"But didn't you find it? You're free now. You can eat whatever you want, sing whatever you want, laugh whenever you want."

"Maybe." She hugged herself. "I still don't understand it. It doesn't make much sense to me."

Her words resonated with me. Anyone who crossed the Tumen under cover of night would understand—foreign countries, unfamiliar tongues, our destitution, the SPSD, snitches, uncaring people walking past, extreme cold and rain, the anxiety of not being able to predict what was to happen—none of this changed just because we were now in Macau.

"I have a lot of debt," Yong-ae confided, lowering her voice. "They wanted a security deposit before I began singing here. The promoter lent me money but the interest is really high and the fee isn't great. I'm making my payments but the debt's growing. I'm never going to be able to leave this place."

"How much do you owe?"

"Fifty thousand dollars. I think. I'm not sure." She wiped her eyes, black mascara streaking one cheek.

I didn't know what to say. I didn't know how to make her feel better.

Later, we left and walked along the wet, warm neon streets before getting into a cab. We stopped at a house on a quiet street in Coloane.

"Is this where you live?" I asked.

She smiled at me. "I don't live anywhere. I just stay here."

That night, I lay curled in her room, swimming through the dark ocean of silence.

THE FAIR GAME OF LIFE

Mr. Oh died. He had committed suicide. Early on the morning of September 8, 2005, Mr. Oh put on a new black suit, combed his hair, and jumped out a window on the thirty-seventh floor of the hotel. He was taken to Saint Memorial Hospital. We sprinted to the hospital as soon as we heard. He had met a lonely end. He hadn't left anything behind.

We talked to the dealer who had seen him last. Mr. Oh had stood up from the table around three in the morning. "He lost his last chip, then sat still for a moment." He shook his head. "He'd had amazing luck earlier. He won $200,000 before ten p.m.!"

Dash's mouth fell open. He shot me a look. "Told you," he mumbled. "You *can* get lucky."

"But luck is what drove him to death," the dealer interjected. "He always got up once he won a hundred bucks, you know? This time, he couldn't help himself. That's what killed him."

I remembered what Mr. Oh had told us, that nobody could win against the house.

"He kept going," the dealer continued. "When that last chip was gone, he pushed his hair back, picked up his empty briefcase, and walked out the door. That's the last time I saw him."

I stamped his death with a prayer. His body would turn into powder before being poured into a ceramic vessel for his flight home to Korea.

"Money's the problem," Dash groused. "If he had money, he wouldn't have died."

I realized then that I needed money, too. I had to buy Yong-ae's freedom. Then she wouldn't have to sing for strangers from a dark stage; she could sing for herself.

✪ ✪ ✪

The casino was a magnet for money from all around the world. Dollars, yen, euros, and yuan joined and became a rainbow of chips, which were thrown down and sucked into slot machines.

Dash stuck his head out from the bottom bunk. "Hey, Gil-mo," he called. "The odds of winning are one out of thirty-six, since there are eighteen black and eighteen red slots. So if you bet a dollar, you get thirty-six bucks back. You lose some, you win some, but those aren't bad odds."

I looked down at him from my bunk. "Those aren't great odds. Don't forget zero. That's the house's. So it isn't thirty-six out of thirty-six, it's thirty-six out of thirty-seven. So each game, you lose one out of thirty-seven, which is around 2.7 percent. Your return is 97.3 percent. So if you bet a hundred bucks, you can only get ninety-seven bucks and thirty cents back. You're done after thirty-seven games."

Dash frowned. "But that's still a good chance, isn't it? Especially if you compare it to buying a lottery ticket. All you have to do is win just once, and you multiply your win by thirty-six."

"But nobody plays a single game," I reminded him. "Betting the same amount each time, if you play two games, your loss ratio is 5.4 percent. Three games? It's 8.1 percent. Ten games is 27 percent, and twenty games is 54 percent. So you end up losing half the money you bet."

"But the probability of winning goes up if you put your money down on two or three numbers at a time. Or even and odd numbers or something."

I shook my head. "If you put chips down on two slots, it's two out of thirty-seven, but you have to split your money up so the win's going to be that much smaller. You lose no matter what you do."

"So what if we bet more?" Dash asked. "Let's say we bet on red but we don't win. So we keep doubling our bet until we win. We'll win big at some point."

"That's impossible. You'd need so much money. And anyway, they put a cap on how much you can bet."

"So you're saying we can never win?" Dash looked frustrated.

"Let's say you're at a casino where the cap is a thousand dollars," I explained. "If you bet ten dollars, then double it each time, by the seventh game you can bet six hundred and forty bucks, but by the eighth game you're over the cap."

"But nobody will be able to stop you if you're really smart about it or really lucky." Dash was stubborn in his belief that luck would come to him and that life was essentially fair. "Probability is exact. If you roll a die, you're guaranteed to win once every six times."

"So you think you'll win once every twelve times if you roll two dice?"

Dash nodded confidently. "Of course."

"But think about this," I countered. "The probability of getting a seven is six times higher than getting a twelve."

"What do you mean?"

"You can only get twelve from a six and a six, right? To get a seven, you can roll a six and a one, a five and a two, a three and a four, a four and a three, a two and a five, or a one and a six. That's six options. What are your odds of getting a one?"

Dash stared at me blankly.

"Zero. You can never roll a one, because you have two dice."

Dash looked crestfallen.

"But there's one other possibility," I said slowly, thinking hard. "It's not a mathematical solution, but maybe the law of physics can help us."

"How?" Dash perked up.

"The thirty-seven slots of a roulette wheel can't be identical. There may be differences in the pockets. Maybe one has a little more give on the bottom or something. But to find the tiniest difference, we'd have to watch the games for several days."

"I'll do it if it's going to make us rich," Dash said excitedly.

"But there's no use if they figure it out . . ."

"So we really can't win against the house, huh?"

His question spun in my head. I shook my head regretfully.

"But you're a math genius," he cried. "Can't you think of something?"

Even I couldn't accurately measure the spin of the wheel or distance. Nor could I compound all the possibilities of a slot machine. The only game we could possibly figure out would be blackjack, since I would be able to predict what cards were left in the deck. But counting cards required a strict division of roles, and I didn't have a team, let alone a partner.

✪ ✪ ✪

In a smart black suit and white shirt, Dash slid his cigar pack into his inner pocket, patting his pants pocket to make sure he had fake IDs for the both of us. The fake IDs he'd confiscated from gamblers as a security guard had come in handy. Each time we went to a new casino in our attempt to find a mathematical solution to our problem, we took new IDs—Matsumoto Yoji from Fukuoka, Richard Chang from Singapore, Nguyen Tha from Vietnam.

I hid behind Dash's wide back, feeling paralyzed in unfamiliar spaces, noise, and crowds. When he put on his fedora and nice clothes, Dash looked ten years older. He could pass for a young businessman or a wealthy scion. At the roulette tables, stone-faced dealers pulled chips toward them and got ready for the next round. Having changed money into $1 chips, Dash placed bets, holding a can of beer in one hand. I observed the mathematical relationship between the wheel, the balls, the dealer, and time. The wheels spun endlessly. The rainy season passed as we did our homework. It was now November.

Dash reassured me every night as we left empty-handed. "This is tuition. We have to invest in this education to get something out of it." Sometimes it sounded as though he were trying to reassure himself.

With no money left, we went to bed without dinner. We had starved in our past lives, but this felt different. The long-forgotten feeling of deprivation clawed our sleep, crushing our dreams. I couldn't come up with a way to win. The statistics I gathered were too irregular to deploy. I had to find a system that would make us win each time.

We stepped into Tomorrow Casino. Dash was wearing a black suit and was chomping on a cigar. The guards checked our IDs. Today, Dash was Richard Chang from Singapore, and I was Wei Zhenmin from Shanghai. We changed $1,000 into chips and went to a roulette table. Dash sat down and placed a bet as I watched from behind. Each time the wheel spun, his chips went to the dealer. Two hours later, he was out. I hesitantly took his seat. The wheel clattered and spun; a hush fell over the table as people watched the balls spinning around. I placed my bet.

"No more bets," the dealer said.

When the wheel stopped, the dealer took all the chips. I glared at the wheel before betting on four numbers. The wheel spun again, and the balls clicked into pockets. People began murmuring. I had won. The dealer kept going, expressionless. Two hours later, I cashed in my chips and left with $2,300. Day after day, I gradually increased my take. Rumors of the boyish gambling phenom spread through the streets of Macau. I was winning small but consistently. People began gathering around me to watch and place their bets with mine.

The problem occurred when the bets began growing. One night, a guard stopped us as we headed toward the roulettes. "Please come with me."

Dash hesitated.

"Don't make this into a bigger problem," the guard said quietly.

Dash followed the guard haughtily, and I followed. Four guards surrounded us as we went down a steep staircase behind a small employees-only bathroom in the corner. A steel door with peeling paint clanged open and they shoved us into a dark room, where a floor manager was waiting for us.

"These are fake IDS," he said. "You aren't Richard Chang and Wei Zhenmin! You're Hu Enlai and Jiang Jiajie. You're a security guard and you're a janitor at Megasquare."

Dash fastened the top button of his jacket. "I'm sure a third of your clients on the floor have showed fake IDs," he shot back. "No gambler wants his true identity known."

The manager squinted at him. "You've been winning consistently. From our perspective—"

Dash cut him short. "Are you accusing us of cheating?"

"Well, your win rate is suspicious."

"We do work at a casino," Dash snapped. "Is that a crime?"

The manager shook his head.

"And we have been winning at roulette. Is that a crime?"

The manager shook his head again.

"Do you have proof that we cheated?"

The manager shook his head once more.

Dash reared back. "Then why are you holding us against our will in this hole?" he thundered. "Maybe I should call the police right now! Or a reporter! What do you think will happen to you if people hear that the Tomorrow holds customers without any evidence and threatens them? I don't doubt that you'll lose your job. And we'll be taking you to court!"

The manager waved his hand in supplication. "No, no, we're not threatening you. I wanted to have a conversation. Your win rate is so high."

"We don't cheat, we're good!" Dash cried.

"But you did enter with fake IDs," the manager countered.

I felt queasy. What if he discovered that we were from North Korea and didn't have official IDs?

"Hear me out first," Dash said, lowering his voice. "Don't you want more customers who stay longer and make more bets?"

The manager narrowed his eyes.

"We're not the enemy," Dash said magnanimously. "We're on your side."

"How do you figure?"

"Where else will you get free publicity for the Tomorrow? All we want is to be able to come here."

The manager cocked his head, looking interested.

"See, this is how it works. People will flock here because we're winning so much. You know that word of mouth is everything." Dash was right. We only won around $3,000 each time. There was no way we could win more than $10,000 even if we increased our bets. But more people would come to watch us, hoping they would also get lucky.

That was how we managed to get the casino to look upon us benevolently. With the buzz, gamblers poured into the Tomorrow from all over Macau, Hong Kong, Singapore, Tokyo, and Shanghai. A group even sprang up to study my bets, though they never figured out my secret. People lost all the money they brought before they had to leave to catch their flights home.

✩ ✩ ✩

The roulette wheel spun and clattered. Everyone glanced at me. I put a $500 chip on black and a $500 chip on odds. Excited that I doubled my usual bet, people followed suit. A huge pile of chips rested on black and on odds.

The dealer dabbed his forehead with a handkerchief. "No one on red?"

Dash spewed cigar smoke and pushed a pile of chips on red. $10,000. He glanced at the dealer and put the same amount on evens. Then Yong-ae placed her bet on red and evens, too: $30,000. She slid a long, thin cigarette in her mouth. Men around her vied to light her cigarette.

"No more bets."

It grew quiet as people wiped sweat off their foreheads. This was turning out to be the biggest game of the day. The wheel slowed gradually and the balls clattered into place. Moans erupted. Only Dash and Yong-ae let out cheers. I lost $1,000, Dash won $20,000, and Yong-ae won $30,000. We ended up with $49,000, and the house earned nearly $300,000. We played two more rounds, losing $20,000 the second time and winning $30,000 the third. We cashed out our chips and left.

We booked a room at the Sofitel Macau to celebrate. Lights twinkled in the ocean outside and sparkled along the streets. We ordered a bottle of Moët and Chandon and popped the cork.

Dash raised his glass. "We're rich!" White bubbles fizzled in his glass as he clinked it against mine.

"We're not rich," I corrected.

"Oh, we're not?" Dash gestured at the shiny briefcase filled with Benjamin Franklin and Ulysses S. Grant.

"That's not ours," I explained calmly. "We're giving it to the manager of the Casablanca. Then Yong-ae can leave the club."

Dash stared at me, then at Yong-ae. "Is that all you care about?" He poured himself another glass. "Fine, we're not rich. At least we can enjoy ourselves tonight. We'll be rich one day. We'll rule Macau, just like Kunlun was king of Shanghai!" He laughed and drank some more champagne.

✩ ✩ ✩

Two days later, we handed $50,000 to the manager of the Casablanca, but he demanded additional interest of $5,000. "What will you do now?" he asked Yong-ae.

"I'm heading to Seoul," she said. "My father dreamed of going there."

The manager nodded. "You should leave as soon as possible. You don't have anywhere to stay anymore." He pulled his chair up to his computer and turned the screen around to show us. It was Dash's face.

Dash gasped, turning ashen.

The manager pressed a key, switching to a photo of me, then Yong-ae. He grinned. "I heard you pulled a big one at the Tomorrow. But now you're on the no-entry list for all the casinos."

We understood—this was why he had absolved Yong-ae of her debt without argument. She couldn't enter his club anyway.

"I'm saying this because Sarah and I worked together and everything," the manager said. "You should be careful. They'll come at you since you won so big. If I were you I'd hide out for a little while."

Dazed, we walked to the wharf, where panhandlers were wandering around luxury yachts. We sat at a colonial-style open-air café. Dash flicked ash off his cigar and gazed at a gull sitting at the end of a mast. "Fifty-five thousand dollars! I knew prices were steep, but that was ridiculous."

Yong-ae crumpled up her employee badge and threw it in the ocean. The white cellophane fluttered into the blue sky, flashing in the afternoon sunlight.

★ ★ ★

"That very incident, the fraudulent gambling at the Tomorrow Casino, put you on the Public Security Police Force of Macau's blacklist," Angela says.

"It wasn't fraudulent gambling."

"Then how could you win so big?"

"All I did was exploit the maggots in the casino," I explain.

"What are you talking about?"

I tell her about the first day we went to the casino with our fake IDs. Dash lost all our chips, and we had to skip dinner. Dash lay in his bunk back home, dejected. "It's going to be impossible to win," he grumbled. "It's a giant food chain. The lion's on top, then the leopard, the elephant and antelope, small rabbits, and finally, mice."

"What?"

"The owner of the casino is the lion. The floor manager, head of security, and guards are small predators. The cashiers and cheaters are crocodiles and hyenas. We're the food."

"Oh. So then who are the maggots?"

"There are no maggots."

"There are always maggots in a food chain," I explained. "They eat the lion's corpse. We can't win when we fight the lion, but maybe we can defeat the maggot."

Dash sat up. "Cashiers and prostitutes!"

"No," I said. "They're more like the hyenas."

Dash twirled his fedora. "Dealers!" he cried. "Some dealers have an understanding with security. They sometimes don't give all the money up, or they siphon the customer's bets at the table. If they're all in on it, they can get away with it. The dealer swipes the cash, the guard looks the other way, the cashier doesn't record that amount. That's why they keep switching everyone's places. They won't prosecute even if a dealer gets away with it. It's bad publicity."

"Really?"

"Why would they advertise that their employees are stealing from the customer?"

That was what we would do. Rotten dealers, guards, and cashiers—we could leverage this.

"What are you thinking?" Dash asked eagerly. "Do you have an idea?"

"We'll do a big spring cleaning," I said cautiously.

The following day, I told Yong-ae all about it.

"Don't do anything stupid," she said. "Keep your head down."

"I'm not going to be stupid. We're ready. We just need $5,000."

"There's no way you can get that kind of money," she scoffed. "Let me get it for you."

"I don't want to drag you into this," I protested.

"You already have. I'm investing. $5,000 is nothing compared to the amount of debt I have."

Dash and I went from casino to casino, studying security guards and dealers. Yong-ae's money funded our research of maggot ecology; soon we discovered a thriving habitat at the roulette table at the Tomorrow. Dash made hundreds of small bets as I examined their tactics and gathered data. Some days we lost a bit of money, but other days we won and raised our stakes.

Angela looks at me suspiciously. "So you wanted to be caught by the floor manager?"

I nod. "Of course. Because that allowed us to come and go as we pleased."

"But it could still be fraudulent gambling," Angela points out. "How else would you win so consistently?"

The wheel spins dizzily before my eyes. "It was simple. We were placing our bets on the least likely number."

"That doesn't make sense," Angela says. "How do you make money by betting on a number nobody is betting on?"

"If someone put $30,000 on black, I would put $1,000 on red."

"But the probabilities don't change," Angela says, looking confused.

"Of course they don't. But what if the dealer wants the $30,000? What happens if he can control the game?"

"Oh . . ." Angela starts nodding. "He would have the ball stop on red."

"They were using electromagnets to move the balls and the roulette wheel," I tell her.

THE DEATH OF A FUGITIVE

Now free, Yong-ae got on a plane to Seoul. Having spent every last penny on Yong-ae's debt, we were destitute. And we couldn't even enter a casino. We moved to a smaller room with mold in the walls. Hunger dogged us as Dash began losing weight again. We had to find work. We couldn't find employment in a legitimate casino, but we were able to find jobs at an illegal casino on the docks. It was a small operation with impressive stakes. People came from all over the world, stimulated by the heightened danger and high risk. The casino received wires over the legal limit and pocketed foreign exchange gains. Dash worked as a security guard and I took over the cage.

Dash pleaded with me every morning. "Let's just do one more game and leave this place. Let's go to Seoul."

I was hesitant, as much as I wanted to go to Seoul. "But we don't really need money. I only wanted to do it to pay back her debt."

"Then why did we come all the way here? To be flat-out broke?"

"We got to be rich," I tried. "We were able to buy Yong-ae's freedom."

Dash's veins popped in his neck. "That selfish bitch? She used you and left us here! We're stuck here because of her!" He yanked his jacket off the hanger and slammed the door on his way out.

He came back a week later, completely transformed. His eyes were sunken, his hair was stiff, and his face was dirty. He flung himself onto his bed. "Gil-mo, you know how much I value you," he began. "Well, it doesn't matter if you don't. I just need you to do me a favor."

I nodded, shocked at the way he looked.

He rubbed his dry lips. "Just one last time," he pleaded. "Then we'll leave."

I stared into the distance, shaking my head. I smoothed my pants with my hands.

Dash sighed. "Look, let me tell you what I've done. I thought I'd do one last round and make enough to leave. So I borrowed $5,000 from the manager and joined a blackjack game. I won a little at first. I should have left. I really should have. I lost everything. So then I borrowed more. It was already going to be impossible to pay it back, so . . . I ended up borrowing $50,000. He cut me off. I'm never going to be able to pay it back. He suggested another way."

"What is it?"

"Three days from now there's going to be a huge blackjack game in the suites at the Four Seasons. Two guys from Saudi Arabia, the heir to the Kowloon Hotel in Hong Kong, and a businessman from Shanghai: $200,000 each."

"So?"

"They want you to play. I didn't realize he lent me the money because of you. I'm supposed to bring you to the game. If not—"

I understood. If I didn't go, Dash would never get away, and he might float up as a half-rotten corpse on the beach. His body might never be discovered. Then how would I be able to deliver his death?

"This will really be the last time," Dash said desperately. "Think about it, it's achieving balance and symmetry. People have so much, and we have nothing. We just have to find the right balance, taking a little money from people who have too much. Then we'll leave. I promise."

I did like balance and symmetry. I picked up a deck of cards and began to shuffle. We had less than seventy-two hours to prepare, and I had to craft a strategy to win against these high rollers.

✪ ✪ ✪

Our black limousine slid to a stop in front of the Four Seasons. Dash, in a black suit and dark sunglasses, wiped the sweat on his forehead. We entered the elevator and pressed 28. A lucky number—the sum of all of its factors except itself came out to 28. I hitched up my knapsack; Dash had insisted I bring it. The doors opened to two men waiting for us. They led us to the suite at the end of the hallway—it had three bedrooms, a meeting room, and an office, and everything smelled pleasant. We were overlooking the ocean. Around the oak card table in the middle of the meeting room sat four people—two men in traditional Saudi clothing and two Asians in suits. The Arabs were cousins of Saudi royalty, gamblers who played extensively in Las Vegas and Monte Carlo. The young businessman from Shanghai was Min Zengzhi, and David Ching was the heir to the Kowloon Hotel fortune. Retired dealer Jolly Cai was standing there; he was renowned for his skillful dealing and high win rate.

I joined them at the table. Everyone took out bundles of cash from bags their bodyguards had carried in and piled them on the table. I took one-hundred-dollar bills out of the bag Dash handed me and stacked them in front of me.

Cai shuffled the cards, sending them dancing around the table. I hunched my shoulders and stared at the cards. Someone offered drinks. David Ching picked something that was on the rocks. The Saudis grabbed non-alcoholic beer, and I asked for Coca-Cola. I was poured a tall, frosted glass of soda. Cards were dealt again. Soon, I was familiar with each of their personalities and the dealer's habits. I could predict the cards in Cai's hands. The men's faces grew tense. Fear hung over us. I wasn't afraid, though. Nor was I tense. This made me the most daring player at the table. Now down a hundred thousand, David was chain smoking. I coughed. The smoke swirling overhead and my cough broke the Saudis' concentration. It was now past six, and David had lost $120,000 and the old Saudi had lost $30,000. The younger Saudi had won $40,000. When I won $50,000, I got up from the table. The manager glanced at the others and requested a short break.

He followed Dash and me as we went into the other room. "What's going on?" he whispered. "You're on a roll."

"I'm done," I said. "Now we're even."

"You're not done," he hissed. "Nobody stops playing until someone wins it all. Not a single bill can move off the table until someone's done. There's only one way for you to pay me back. Win the whole pot, and I'll write off your friend's debt."

"That wasn't the deal!" Dash said hotly.

"We have to follow the rules of this room," the manager snapped. "If you try to leave now, who knows what those guys will do to you."

We were stuck. We had to continue and try to take the whole pot. I went back to the table. David lost his calm and began to make increasingly risky moves. The stakes grew larger, and even the Saudis, who had remained cool throughout, began to lose their composure. It was dark now, but the cards kept going around. Shuffle, deal, count, bet, split, deal, count, bet. David was drunk. The Saudis began to increase their bets, only to be defeated in the last hand. Around eleven p.m., most of the cash had moved; it was in front of me. David had folded a while ago and was now passed out in the bedroom. The younger Saudi gave the rest of his cash to his cousin and folded. The goddess of fate was on my side. The older Saudi was out after two hands. Min Zengzhi soon lost the rest of his cash; the game was over.

Dash packed two bags full of cash. The manager watched contentedly. The day's game could be summed up with a simple formula: $200,000 \times 4 - 50,000 = 0$. The four others had lost $200,000 each, I had won $800,000, Dash had paid back his $50,000, and the manager had made $750,000. We were left with nothing.

Two black limousines were waiting for us in front of the hotel. The manager carried the bags and got in the car in the rear. I got in after him. Dash sat in the passenger seat. The guard car in front led the way out of the hotel driveway. We merged onto the dark shoreline road.

The manager shifted his gaze from the bags to me, then to Dash, grinning widely.

"Didn't I tell you he's amazing?" crowed Dash.

The manager took out a small bottle of whiskey from the bar and downed it. "He's an animal! We're going to be great partners."

I stared out at the black ocean gliding by outside.

Dash's voice hardened. "We paid you back. We're done. I promised him."

The manager threw back some more whiskey and shook his head. "Trust me, you're going to like this. You'll be rich soon enough. Did you know that people line up to ask me to back them? I've chosen this guy here. You should both be grateful."

Dash looked helpless.

The manager's grin froze and he whipped around to look behind him. "The Shanghai assholes are tailing us."

We looked back. Two black cars were speeding toward us. Our driver gunned the gas and they followed suit. The manager called the escort car ahead of us. One of the black cars changed lanes, sped up, and cut us off. The brakes screamed and I lurched forward. Our escort car slowed down, but it was already quite far ahead of us. Four men got out of the black car that had cut us off. They pulled their guns out. The manager took a gun out of the middle console. Our escorts ran toward us, shooting. Three of them fell but they did get two of the assailants. Our front window shattered and the driver slumped forward.

"Step on it!" yelled the manager. "We need to get out of here!"

Dash pushed the driver out of the way and squeezed into the driver's seat. He picked up the driver's gun and stepped on the gas. The car shot forward with a roar. The manager ducked and fired through the broken back window as Dash began shooting out of his window while careening along the road. The gunshots grew fainter.

The manager regained his smirk and leaned back. "See? I told you we'd be a fantastic team."

His phone rang; it was one of his colleagues. The manager explained what had happened and directed him to find us. "You can track my car's GPS," he said, and hung up.

Dash halted the car with a screech.

"What are you doing?" shouted the manager. "Keep driving!"

Without a word, Dash turned around and pointed his gun at the manager, whose face drained of color. Dash pulled the trigger. The blast was muffled under the sound of waves crashing. Warm blood spurted out of the manager's chest and splattered my face. I screamed out the window: "He's dead!"

Dash reached behind and grabbed me by the throat. "Shut up, Gil-mo!" he hissed. "We would never have been able to get away as long as he was alive."

The lights along the winding road danced on the water. "But... but you're not a murderer!"

"Nobody's born a murderer," Dash snapped. "You only become one once you kill someone." He took out two bundles of cash from one of the bags and shoved them in my jacket pockets. "Go to the port. There's a boat called *Yellow Marine* at the docks. Tell the guy there that Richard Chang sent you. Give him a thousand dollars, and he'll take you to the Hong Kong ferry docks. Go to the Hong Kong International Airport." He took out an envelope from his inner pocket. He showed me an airplane ticket. "We have seats on the 2:20 p.m. flight to Seoul tomorrow." He took his own ticket out and showed me. "You have the window seat. I have to tie up some loose ends here. I'll see you on the plane tomorrow." He studied me before pulling me in for a hug.

He smelled like sweat and blood. I squirmed but he wouldn't let go. To distract myself, I counted the knobs of his spine with a finger. I counted up to twelve. Suddenly a screech of tire. Dash shoved me away and put the car into gear. "Run, Gil-mo. To the harbor. Okay?"

I hesitated. I rubbed my thighs.

"Did you hear me? Get lost!" shouted Dash. "What are you, stupid?"

I didn't answer. I didn't know what to do.

Dash's voice turned gentle. "Gil-mo, I'm sorry. You're not stupid. People who call you stupid are the stupid ones." He smiled.

I nodded. He leaned across me to fling open my door. Salty wind rushed into the car. He shoved me out. I landed on my stomach on the warm asphalt and watched as he revved the engine and disappeared around the corner. Everything smelled like exhaust. I got up and stumbled toward the harbor. A black sedan came roaring down the street toward me. It had to be the car following our limo's GPS signal. I began to run. Dash didn't kill the manager by accident, I realized. He had already arranged for a boat to Hong Kong. He had bought plane tickets. And he had told me to bring my knapsack. This was all so reckless. Cars screeched at a distance and something crashed. I heard gunshots. It grew quiet. I ran even faster. I was at the docks. I looked for the yellow boat.

✩ ✩ ✩

I sat in my seat, 23A, on the Korean Air flight to Incheon. The seat next to mine was still empty. Passengers entered, but I didn't see Dash. Soon, everyone was on board. Three people rushed on at the last minute. The flight attendants helped them put their bags away and checked to ensure that everyone was seated and buckled in. Still, the seat next to mine was unoccupied. The plane pushed off and rolled onto the runway. With a roar, the scene outside the window shot past, making me dizzy. The vibration of the wheels on the ground ceased and the runway grew smaller. I was flying. Sunlight streamed in through my small window.

"Would you like a newspaper?" A flight attendant was smiling at me, a dimple in her cheek.

I selected the *South Asia Morning Post*. The headline jumped out at me. OVERNIGHT SHOOTOUT BETWEEN ILLEGAL GAMBLING RINGS ON SHORELINE ROAD IN MACAU. I read on. *The Public Security Police Force of Macau announced that a shootout had occurred on the shoreline road in Macau last night. Seven died and four were injured. Five bodies were recovered, all killed by a .38-caliber revolver. Three abandoned cars were found near the bodies. Another car 1.5 kilometers away from the scene*

*contained the bodies of illegal gambling tycoon Can Xiahong
and an associate. Police believe that they were killed during
their escape from the main shootout. Conflicts between illegal
gambling rings occur frequently, resulting in murders, bomb-
ings, shootings, and attacks on police. In recent years, a con-
certed campaign against illegal gambling has helped reduce
such incidents. Police are investigating the whereabouts of
gang members suspected of fleeing the scene.*

My eyes slid over to the photograph of the scene. Cars rid-
dled with bullets, bloodstains on the asphalt, shattered glass.
The driver's seat of our limousine soaked in blood. Next were
headshots of the dead. Dash was there, smiling, next to six
others. My friend, who ate to compensate for his past, who was
dogged by hunger, who wanted to be a novelist and spin tales
that sounded true, was dead. I wanted to wipe his fat face and
scarred body with cotton balls and deliver his death. Instead,
I rubbed his smiling face in the paper with my palm, smearing
the ink. I knew I would need a lot of stamps for him, since he
was so heavy; I didn't stop praying for a long time.

I opened my eyes. Clouds billowed outside the window.
Dash was looking in. He was flying, smiling happily. "Dash,
isn't it hard to fly next to the plane?"

He shook his head and flapped his wings.

"You went exactly how you wanted to, just like Chow Yun-
fat in his movies." He had known how he wanted to die, though
he hadn't figured out how he wanted to live.

"I did. I aimed at the bad guys and got shot. Just like Chow
Yun-fat." Dash flew up higher and higher. My plane began
drifting down toward Earth. I looked down at the roofs of
Seoul. I was here now. Somewhere, Yong-ae was here, too.

✪ ✪ ✪

"That's a lovely dream. Your friend was with you even then," Angela says.

"That wasn't a dream," I correct her. "Dash was flying next to the plane. We talked."

"A person can't fly," Angela says.

"Are you saying I'm lying?"

"Or maybe you hallucinated."

"He flew next to me. He talked to me, then he flew up higher."

Angela just stares at me.

I know there is magic in the world. People only believe in things they can see, but invisible things exist, too. Numbers tell you everything you need to know about physics, music, even poetry and philosophy. "I'll prove to you that magic and miracles exist," I say hotly.

She shakes her head gently. "Please stop. I can't help you if you're like this." She's still suspicious of me. I can't say that I blame her.

DAY SIX: SEOUL

February 2006–August 2007

★

Interpol Red Notice: Ahn Gil-mo
Wanted by the judicial authorities of Korea,
Republic of, for prosecution / To serve a sentence
Charges: Fraud

In 2002, Ahn Gil-mo defected from North Korea and passed through Yanji, Shanghai, and Macau before entering South Korea in 2006. He subsequently received Korean citizenship and support from the South Korean government. Authorities discovered that he was a person of interest implicated in hundreds of incidents of fraud, along with two accomplices, also defectors, one of whom was imprisoned for spying. Ahn was suspected of cyber dealing, manipulating stocks, and disturbing the financial markets. After pocketing a large profit, he came under notice of the stock crime unit and was investigated; he also committed additional major crimes and fled overseas. In November 2007, he was placed on the Red Notice.

Another official document from Interpol confirms yet another crime. Banks lobs questions at me, but I remain silent. He asks his question, notes my silence, and moves onto the next. "Did you cross illegally into the United States?"

I don't answer.

"This is ridiculous!" he snaps. "Even a Red Notice criminal can refuse to answer any questions."

Angela comes in, holding a thermometer and a chart. Banks sighs and leaves the room. Angela takes my temperature and draws blood. I scribble a poem of my own making.

I wish I could calculate my mystical dream.

3.14159265

She puts the chart down and writes:

The shiny daylight reflects unknown yearnings.

358979

We take turns writing down the value of pi.

"What did he ask you?" Angela asks casually.

I don't answer.

"Why don't we focus on the fraud you committed in Seoul? And the manipulation of stock prices?"

"I didn't manipulate stocks. I just bought suitable stocks at the right time and sold them at the right time."

"Tell me what happened," Angela suggests.

I go back to the day I arrived in Seoul.

SIX DEGREES OF SEPARATION

I left Incheon International Airport and made my way to Seoul Station. Years ago, I had read an article to Kunlun about the homeless people congregating there. I figured that was the perfect place for me, since I also didn't have a home. I placed my knapsack in a coin locker and ate free meals given out by volunteers. About a week in, a volunteer asked me where I was from and where my family was. I told her that I was from Pyongyang, that I arrived via Shanghai and Macau, and that my parents were dead. Her eyebrows shot up in surprise. She ladled extra soup for me that day. But before I could finish my lunch, police surrounded me and put me in a squad car. They photographed me and asked endless questions. Finally, they figured out that I wasn't Chinese, Macanese, or Japanese, but North Korean. I was handed over to investigators specializing in defectors. They peppered me with questions. Where did I live in Pyongyang? Where were my parents? How did I get to China? What did I do in Macau? I told them about my life in Pyongyang, the prison camp, Yanji, Shanghai, and Macau. They seemed to suspect that I was an ethnic Korean with Chinese citizenship from Yanji, trying to enter South Korea as a defector, aiming for a citizen's ID and resettlement funds provided to North Koreans. They were professionals at ferreting out fake defectors. With ten thousand defectors living in South Korea, one out of every two thousand North Koreans, a defector would know at least one or two people from back home.

A few days later, the investigator closed his file. "We found someone who knows you. Once we can verify your identity, you will become a South Korean citizen."

Later, I was told that this person had arrived. I combed my hair carefully and went to the visiting area, which contained three tables with two chairs on each side. The door opened, and I looked up eagerly, expecting to see Yong-ae.

"Gil-mo!" he called, striding over to give me a tight embrace. He patted me jovially on the back.

I extricated myself and stared at him, at his asymmetrical face, his drooping, shiny skin, his gold-rimmed glasses, his comb-over. His fleshiness and glasses obstructed the face I had known, but it came to me: Yun Yong-dae, the warden at Muryong prison camp.

"So do you know this young man?" asked the investigator.

"Yes, yes! This is Ahn Gil-mo. He was at my camp for two years." He smiled warmly. "Welcome to Seoul, Gil-mo! Don't worry about anything. I'll look after you. I know that's what your poor father would have wanted."

But I was supposed to look after Yong-ae. "Do you know where Yong-ae is?" I asked.

"That's right, you left the camp because of her," exclaimed the warden. "I'll help you find her. You'll have a good life here, Gil-mo. I'll help you. You'll make money, find Yong-ae, and live a nice life."

After the warden left, the investigator marveled at my luck. "Mr. Yun is a model case," he said. "If all defectors were like him we'd be out of a job. He's adapted to Korean society very well. He's quite comfortable, and he's become a Christian, you know."

He had become a Christian? But my father was put in the prison camp for a single Bible. He perished there, and I didn't know where my mother had gone. Christianity had made me an orphan.

The investigator blathered on, not noticing my shock. "Mr. Yun began taking care of other defectors. He founded an organization called Defector Friendship Collective. He gives talks about how horrible life is under communism. He became well known in the community, and government agencies work with him closely now. It's an amazing story, really, considering that he crossed the border without anything on him. You're in good hands. He'll give you all the tools you need to be a contributing citizen, just like him."

I sat still, stunned. I didn't understand why a loyal official of the republic left. And how did a warden of a prison camp come to sponsor defectors, the likes of whom he used to treat like animals? Could he have become a better man?

✪ ✪ ✪

I was sent to Hanawon, a resettlement center for defectors. My room had a small desk, a fan, and a drying rack for laundry. The warden bustled around, making sure the boiler was working and I had hot water. He promised he'd be back soon. From my window, I watched his black car drive out of the parking lot. He was so kind now. The Heavenly Father had to be a good person if he was able to change the warden into such a nice man.

The resettlement education curriculum was 420 hours over twelve weeks. It taught us about cultural differences between the two Koreas, sought to develop democratic civic consciousness and cultivate societal and economic independence, instructed us with basic job skills, provided psychological support, and made sure we were adjusting. Every week, the warden visited me with an armload of books. Perhaps this was his way of compensating for all the horrible things he had done to me in the camp. I didn't want his silent apologies, but I eagerly awaited the books. Through them, I understood more about Seoul, South Korea, democracy, and capitalism.

Three months later, I left Hanawon. It was summer. I walked out of the facility with a new bag filled with all my new books. The flowerbeds along the sidewalks were a riot of color. Hot air was thick around me.

A car honked behind me. I turned around. A tinted window slid down. "Congratulations!" called the warden. "You're a South Korean now." He opened a can of Coke and handed it to me as he helped me into his car.

I asked him to take me to Seoul Station. My knapsack in the coin locker had been collected because it had been in there for too long. My head buzzed; the ground shifted. Inside were Knight Miecher's notebook, my calculator, compass, triangles, ruler, tape measure, buttons of different colors, and fake passports. The warden reached through the fog of my panic and dragged me to the long-term lost-and-found counter. The employee told me I was lucky; my knapsack would have been thrown out if I had come any later. The warden paid the associated fees for me, and I was able to leave with my knapsack.

We stopped at the entrance to a dark, dank alley, dotted with potholes and sour-smelling puddles. Red neon signs in Chinese and Arabic blinked over stores. I followed the warden up a long slope. One hundred and twenty-eight steps later, we had climbed up thirty-eight steep stone steps.

"People here like tall buildings," the warden said, panting. He pushed open a blue galvanized steel gate, revealing a shabby two-story house with many doors. In one corner of the yard was a faucet and a dented basin.

Two men were perched on the small veranda playing go. They didn't bother looking up. The warden climbed up a creaky steel staircase on the side of the house and went up to the roof, where a single room was on top. He opened the door. "Here we are," he announced. "You like it?"

My new home was twenty-four square meters, composed of sixteen square meters of living space and eight square meters for the kitchen and bathroom. People from all over the world lived here. On the first floor was a young Pakistani couple—Ali worked as an assistant night guard at a construction site and Shareen worked at a restaurant with her pregnancy under wraps. Shareen went to work when Ali came home, and when she came home, Ali had already left for his job. Next door to them was Purba, a Nepalese laborer, who pretended to be fine at work but moaned all night from various aches and pains. Three Korean girls lived in a single room together; Ji-na, Se-ran, and Su-min, who went to the salon around three in the afternoon for their hair and makeup and returned home at dawn. Su-min told me that if I came to visit her at work with my resettlement funds, she'd show me a good time. On the second floor were Hyon-su and Jong-hye, from Yanjin, who lived next to Mr. Jang and Mr. Cho, laborers in their fifties, the go players, and a middle-aged woman who worked as a cashier in a big box store thirty minutes away.

I settled into life in my small room on the leaky green roof in that noisy, stinky alley. Hyon-su and Jong-hye fought loudly; Su-min yelled, "Keep it down, don't you two ever sleep?"; and Ali and Shareen listened to ABBA. Purba hummed Nepalese tunes, and the cashier lady clanged the dishes together as she washed them. Pigeons cooed around the faucet in the yard. Ali and Shareen's room smelled like bread, while Purba's smelled like instant ramen. Mr. Cho and Mr. Jang argued and bickered. The yard smelled pungent, of kimchi and spicy curry. Perched on top of everything, I looked down at the streets of Seoul spread out below my rusted staircase, the steep hill, and the thirty-eight stone steps.

The warden told me that he placed my resettlement funds in a five-year fixed deposit account with 5.6 percent interest. In five years, I would have just over 30 million won.

Seoul was enormous and plentiful. The asphalt on the streets sparkled in the sun, and even the floors in public restrooms shined. But you could find poverty and discrimination if you looked closely beyond the glitter. According to the warden, South Korea was ten times more complicated than the republic. I should be careful, as someone would take advantage of me if I didn't pay attention. He handed me a pamphlet. "The government is helping defectors settle in by offering classes. There are computer classes or cooking classes or a number of other kinds. Why don't you take some classes?"

"Can I go to cooking school and learn how to make sushi?"

"Sushi? What for?"

"I like rice."

"You can take whatever class you want," the warden said. "You'll get 116,000 won each month for transportation and food while you're enrolled. If you complete more than 500 hours, you get an additional 1.2 million won as an incentive. And if you go on to get a national technical qualification certificate, you get 2 million won. That means you can get up to 3.78 million in addition to your resettlement funds. I'll put any extra funds you get from the government in your savings account so you can make more money."

"I don't want to be rich."

"Here, you do. You work hard, use your head, and make money. You have to be smart, Gil-mo."

I signed up for Japanese cookery. I didn't take classes to

become rich; I knew I would meet more defectors, and that I might bump into someone who knew where Yong-ae was. I believed in numbers and in six degrees of separation. Someone had to have seen Yong-ae after she got here. I showed Yong-ae's picture to an older defector named Min-su, who had worked in the Hamhung mines and sneaked across the river. "How are you going to find someone in this huge city with only a single picture?" he asked.

I explained to him the theory of six degrees of separation.

He laughed, revealing missing teeth. "I wouldn't worry about that, kid."

"What should I worry about?"

"About how to survive! You risked your life to land here. Don't you want to prove to everyone that you can thrive?"

That night, the warden stopped by with a gift—a new computer.

"Thank you," I said. "I can look up academic papers from the School of Mathematics at the Institute of Advanced Study."

"Oh, don't bother with that nonsense," the warden said. "Do something more productive with your time." He typed something into the browser window and hit Enter. Thousands of numbers, graphs, and red and blue arrows climbed and dipped, creating hyperbolas of gains and losses. "This is a stock investment site," he explained. "This is the best place to play with numbers. Mark my words, this is going to be your favorite site."

I peered closer at the screen. A world composed of numbers moved according to invisible but precise rules, driving capitalism on. In my small, shabby rooftop room, I began playing with capitalism's huge engine.

It was still morning, but my rooftop room was sweltering under the heat of the sun. The warden climbed the stairs and rested for a moment outside my open door, wiping his sweaty forehead with a handkerchief. He took out a bundle of documents from his briefcase. "Good news, Gil-mo! Your paternal grandfather is alive here in Seoul!"

I shook my head. "My grandfather died in Haeju on April 28, 1976. April 28 is the one hundred and eighteenth day on the Gregorian calendar. On that date in history, Charles de Gaulle stepped down; General Yi Sun-sin, Saddam Hussein, and Kurt Gödel were born; and iTunes began service."

The warden was staring at me. He must not know who Kurt Gödel was. "Gödel announced what he called the incompleteness theorem in 1931. It suggests that mathematics can't prove its own incompleteness—"

"Never mind that," the warden interrupted. "The date isn't important."

"Father prayed each year on April 28," I prattled on. "So that was clearly the day my grandfather—"

The warden cut me off, exasperated. "That's why I said your grandfather was alive. The man who died in Haeju wasn't your grandfather."

I stared at him.

"I did some research. Your grandfather left your pregnant grandmother in 1950, during the war, and defected to the

South alone. He told her he would be back soon, but with the demilitarized zone established, they were forever torn apart."

"That's not what Father told me. He never told me that my grandfather defected."

The warden tutted. "Of course he didn't. Why would he want to reveal that his mother remarried? Or maybe he didn't know the truth himself." He plucked out a few photographs from the bundles of paper. "This is your grandfather. You won't believe how much work it was to get these photos of him."

I stared at the picture of the old man. His face contained the golden ratio in the width of his forehead, the distance between his eyes and nose, the length of his lips, the space between his brows, the length and width of his eyes. He had white hair, wrinkles revealing life's turns, and a faint smile. Father died before he was able to grow this old. If he lived that long, would he have had this old man's face?

"Aren't the similarities uncanny?" continued the warden. "You both have slightly wavy hair, and the tips of your noses droop a bit."

I could see some similarities, but that didn't mean he was my grandfather. I didn't know what to think. After all, I'd never had one. "Does it matter that this is my grandfather?"

"Yes, of course. It's very important. Because now, you're very, very rich."

None of this meant anything to me.

"Listen carefully, Gil-mo," the warden said seriously. "Your grandfather earned quite a lot of money in the last fifty years. He remarried and had two daughters and a son, but he never forgot his first wife and son up north. Every time the government organized a family reunion, he applied. He never got picked, though. When he heard that I helped defectors get news of their families back home, he contacted me. He asked me to find his first wife. I unfortunately had to bring him the sad news that she remarried and died a long time ago. So he asked about his son. Your father is unfortunately already dead, but I was at least able to find his grandson!"

"I don't want to be rich."

"You're a good kid, Gil-mo. You're smart. Listen carefully, okay? Your grandfather felt guilty his entire life about leaving his wife and son behind. There aren't that many days left ahead for him. You're his only blood relative from North Korea. The portion of his estate meant for his first wife and son would go to you. Gil-mo, it's an enormous amount. Even considering his South Korean family's portion! Think about it. Wouldn't it be a kind thing to relieve him of his guilt? Wouldn't that help him go to heaven in peace, when it's time?"

I understood. It was important to deliver any death, to clean the dead's face and put a stamp of prayer on. Of course I wanted the same for my newfound grandfather. I agreed to go for a visit.

✪ ✪ ✪

My grandfather sat in a shiny silver wheelchair, gazing into the distance. He was pale, quiet, and slow. The sprinklers swished every few seconds, showering the geometric garden in large arcs. A lawyer stood next to the old man. The warden took out a bundle of documents, attesting to my identity, my family history, and where I lived in North Korea. The lawyer examined the documents then whispered something into my grandfather's ear.

"Say hello to your grandfather," the warden murmured, smiling.

I bowed.

Grandfather looked at me with cloudy gray eyes shrouded by damp eyelashes. He took out a faded photograph from his white linen jacket. His pregnant first wife was looking out resentfully. He looked between me and the picture. He put it back in his pocket slowly and stared at me. Grandfather's hazy pupils trembled. Was he disappointed that I wasn't how he'd imagined?

"I'm different," I blurted out. "I live in my own world."

"I see," Grandfather said haltingly, tears rolling down his face. "Everyone's different in some way, and some people don't even know how they're different." His gaze was warm, and I closed my eyes, basking in the warmth.

After that day, the warden and I went to Grandfather's every Tuesday and Thursday. We spent the afternoon there, looking out at the quiet garden.

"Tell me a story," Grandfather said to me one day.

"What kind of story?"

"Any story. About your father, or about you."

To me, stories were something old people told the young. It made sense, since they had seen and heard a lot. I supposed I also saw and heard a lot, even though I was young. I told him about running along the Taedong to see the USS *Pueblo*, about the senior colonel, Kunlun's large grandfather clock, the slot machines at Megasquare, and the satellite I launched, still orbiting in space.

"That was just an image in the mass games," Grandfather corrected me gently. "It didn't really go into orbit."

"It did," I told him. "It launched into the sky and entered orbit, all according to my calculations."

Grandfather looked at me for a moment. "Memories play tricks sometimes. Things that didn't really happen are remembered as though they did. Small occurrences can feel like amazing events. I can see your grandmother, even now, the way she was standing there as I left."

I wanted to prove that I wasn't lying. That night, I brought him out to the garden.

"What is it?" asked Grandfather. "Why do you want me to come out here?"

"I want you to see my satellite." I pointed up at the sky. "The North Star appears near the end of the Big Dipper. But it's actually about seven times farther away."

Grandfather looked up.

"And the star to its right is the Kwangmyongsong-1. That's the satellite I launched. The orbit is 128 degrees southeast due north right now."

Grandfather frowned straining to see. My satellite was small, almost invisible; it was a faint red. He shook his head.

"Father used to say to me that it isn't important whether something really happened or not. It's more important to believe that it did."

Grandfather turned to look at me.

✪ ✪ ✪

Grandfather seemed to believe that our family's misfortune was his doing. He felt increasingly guilty, and as that feeling grew, the portion of my inheritance grew along with it. The more time I spent with him, the more his family grew upset. They had never welcomed me with open arms, but they grew overtly hostile. His son began arguing with him in front of me. "Father, you're being conned!" he cried. "Who knows who this kid really is? That crook Yun Yong-dae is toying with your emotions. He knows how much you miss your family up north."

Grandfather waved his cane to stop him. "That boy is

definitely my grandson! Don't you dare stop him from visiting me."

When they couldn't persuade him otherwise, his children offered a compromise. "Let's take a DNA test," his son suggested. "We can determine for certain whether he's related to us."

Grandfather shook his head in annoyance. "There's no need for any of that. He's already proven himself."

"How could he possibly have done that?"

"With stories."

"Stories? What goddamn stories?"

"My stories," Grandfather retorted. "Things I told my wife before I left. I rubbed her belly as she was wrapping three rice balls for me to take. She was worried we would be parting forever. I took her hand and reassured her that it wasn't important whether we meet again or part forever; I told her what was most important was believing we would see each other again. That was the last thing I told her. Could my son have overheard us? Because fifty years later, that same story came out of that boy's mouth."

His son scoffed. "That's no proof! The kid probably just said whatever popped into his head. You may have told him that story without realizing it!"

"I've never told anyone that story until just now. My first wife is the only one who knew that story. Maybe she told my son that, and then he . . ."

"Father, get a grip on yourself," the son hissed. "These crooks are trying to take your money with these ridiculous stories."

"These aren't ridiculous stories," snapped Grandfather. "A story remains even after someone dies. Don't you see? It's all I have left of my first wife."

✪ ✪ ✪

The warden grinned as he told me the news that I wouldn't need to undergo a DNA test. He and Grandfather's lawyer began to prepare the inheritance paperwork. By the time everything was finalized, the grass was no longer green, and the wind blew dry, brown leaves around. Grandfather died. I prayed in front of his body, clad in brown hemp clothing and laid out in a white room, hoping he would be delivered safely to heaven. I hoped he would meet his first wife and son there.

The warden became my legal guardian because I was still a minor. "Such a generous man," he whispered. "I'm sure he's gone to heaven." Grandfather had left me a little over 200 million won, mostly in bank accounts and some in mutual funds. The warden promised he would oversee the funds and invest it wisely until I turned twenty, the age of adulthood in South Korea.

★ ★ ★

Angela cocks her head. "A satellite reflects sunlight like a star, that's true. But it moves so quickly that it's got to be nearly impossible to see with the naked eye."

"No," I say. "In the middle of the night, the satellite is in the shadow of the earth. Before sunset or sunrise, you can see satellites that shine from the light they get from earth. When the USSR launched Sputnik 1, many people saw it with their naked eye in the early evening and early morning. They would see a bright dot speeding among the other stars in the sky."

"Even so, what you were looking at with your grandfather wasn't a satellite. It was probably a different star. Or a meteor or passing airplane."

"Kwangmyongsong-1 never moves," I correct her. "It's always in that same spot."

"It may look like it's always in the same spot because it's in the same orbit as earth, but it's at 35,810 kilometers above the equator. Without a telescope or binoculars, you just can't see it."

"We saw it that day."

"Fine," Angela finally acquiesces. "If it's important for you to believe you did."

"I can show you where it's going to be tonight. I just have to calculate its orbit."

She nods but she still looks suspicious. "If you're telling the truth, then why did they want you for fraud?"

"After Grandfather died, his family accused us of committing fraud."

"What exactly was the charge?"

"They said we deceived Grandfather, and claimed that he was feebleminded and unable to make decisions. They said we stole part of their inheritance."

"And what's the spying charge about?"

I think back to Seoul, 2006.

CAN YOU HEAR THE SOUND OF TIME PASSING?

Mr. Jang and Mr. Cho were sitting on the narrow veranda and playing go. The cashier lady was doing laundry, while Su-min and the other girls flounced around in short skirts. The men sneaked glances at them from time to time. I still hadn't heard any news of Yong-ae. Seoul wasn't small like Macau. What was the probability that I would find her among ten million people? I wondered what she was doing. She must have achieved her wishes to have a wealthy, fabulous life. I could still feel a centrifugal force binding the connection between us. I felt this tug even when I sat on the veranda in the sun, even when I looked at other girls. Where was she? How had she changed? It turned out I didn't have to wonder for much longer. One day, I spotted her picture in the paper that Mr. Cho was reading.

Female Spy Embedded in Seoul Exposed

A female spy disguised as a defector was caught contacting military generals and government workers for secrets. The joint investigation headquarters composed of the military intelligence unit, National Intelligence Service, and the investigative agency announced that 22-year-old Yun Mi-ra was charged with violating the National Security Law for handing secrets over to the North Korean government. One Captain Lee, age 27, was charged with providing classified information while dating the suspect.

Yun, a spy working for the North Korean State Political Security Department, entered the country in 2005 via Macau and approached Lee and several others under the pretext of romantic interest. She confessed to giving her handlers information she obtained from them and receiving operational funds and orders from the North. Yun also gave twenty-odd talks, spreading Northern propaganda, including that its nuclear development is for its own use, and smuggling out sensitive documents about military unit locations and the settlement of defectors.

Investigator Kim Dal-hwa of the joint investigation headquarters said, "We found it suspicious that Yun dated military personnel and government workers, obtaining documents. After an extensive internal investigation, we were able to bring charges of espionage."

Yong-ae was smiling in the photograph. Her face still contained the golden ratio. I didn't know whether to be happy that I had found her or shocked that she had become a spy.

Mr. Jang and Mr. Cho continued to place their black and white stones on the go board. Black and white, opposites—life, too, was composed of opposites—smiles and tears, joy and sorrow, meeting and parting, love and hate, truths and lies. All of this formed a life. I ruminated on this for a while as Mr. Jang and Mr. Cho continued their game, the stones clacking on the board as chrysanthemum flowers faded in the yard.

✪ ✪ ✪

The warden's car drove down an unfamiliar street and stopped under a tall wall topped with black CCTV cameras. Disoriented,

I was sucked through the enormous steel gates. Twelve minutes later, the warden tapped me on the shoulder and pushed me toward the peeling door of the visiting room. Another door opened on the other side of the glass partition. Yong-ae walked in, wearing a white long-sleeved shirt and loose sweatpants. Her face was clean, without a trace of makeup. I was reminded of the first day we met. The wind was blowing snow off branches, and the ground was black under half-melted snow.

"You've become famous," I said. "Your picture in the paper was huge."

She laughed, making me smile. "It's better to be a famous villain than to have a boring life, isn't it?"

I avoided her gaze and looked down at the small pendant necklace hanging at her throat.

She followed my gaze and smiled. "The only thing my father left me," she said, touching the gold.

She didn't look worried. Was she—was she excited?

"I won't be in prison long," she said in a low voice, leaning forward.

"What will you do?"

"You can sell anything in this country. Anything from knowledge and skills to lies to liquor. I wouldn't have any problem selling my dirty underwear if I could make money off it." She winked.

"What did you sell them to get those secrets?" I whispered.

She thought for a moment. "My past. Also my trust and vulnerability." She paused. "But never my dreams."

"What are they?"

"I'll tell you when I get out of this place."

I didn't doubt that she would leave this place soon. I knew she could make her dreams come true.

✪ ✪ ✪

I felt trapped while Yong-ae was imprisoned. I thought about her constantly. To distract myself, I turned on my computer and went to a stock market site, watching tame numbers appear on the screen. Through graphs and tables, I herded them to a meadow by a calm stream. They listened to me and grazed where I directed them. If I fed them the right kind of interest rates and stocks, they ballooned; if I fed them the wrong kind, they shrank. I looked down at the hazy city from my room at night, listening to the roar of time passing. I thought of what I had lost and gained and of the people who were no longer with me. I watched over my growing flock resting in my blue account books. I was good at this. My numbers grew, multiplying.

"Gil-mo, you're practically a genius," the warden praised.

"I'm not practically a genius," I said. "I *am* a genius."

He laughed, his features turning soft. "Yes, of course. You most certainly are a genius. Even fund managers with ten years' experience wouldn't be able to get such good results. You're our great hope, Gil-mo. You're a North Korean but you'll become richer than most South Koreans!"

I looked over the big numbers printed in my account book. "I'm just growing numbers."

"Right," the warden said heartily. "It's all just numbers. Take good care of them." He reached over to pat my head.

I darted away.

"Sorry, sorry. I forgot. I'm just so proud of you."

✪ ✪ ✪

Six months later, Yong-ae was released on probation after trial. The cashier lady handed me a block of tofu as I headed out to pick her up. "You feed tofu to people who leave prison," she explained. "It's to wipe the slate clean and start over. Blank, like tofu, you see?"

Would my life have turned out differently if I had eaten tofu the night I escaped from the camp?

Just outside the gates of the prison, Yong-ae took a bite of the tofu I handed over. She gave it back to me. Her red lipstick had left a mark on the soft white mass. I took a bite, too. She took another mouthful. White curds bloomed in our dark mouths.

"I want to go to America," she told me.

I couldn't understand her. "But we're citizens of South Korea now," I said, puzzled. "We won't be able to communicate there. They'll look down on us."

"We're second-rate citizens here anyway," Yong-ae retorted. "It's foreign here, too. We can't really communicate, and people look down on us. At least I won't hear them cursing at me or know when they're taking advantage of me if I don't understand what they're saying. There's more freedom there."

"How do you know?"

"The Statue of Liberty is in New York. That's where I'm going to go. So I can look up at her every day." She had a faraway look on her face. She turned and pulled me into a hug; I couldn't breathe.

MY BODY, CARVED BY TIME

A week later, I discovered that my bank account had been drained. The many zeros had disappeared; a sole zero was left behind. This disobeyed all mathematical principles. I looked into the account details; all of my numbers had been taken out in a single withdrawal. I called the warden but he didn't pick up.

When I told Mr. Cho and the cashier lady, they ran to the bank with me. A teller in a navy suit told me it would be hard to recover the money, but that I should file an official report. Mr. Cho took me to the police station. A balding detective in a shapeless jacket combed his hair over his pate. "You're saying over 500 million won disappeared from his account? Then shouldn't we focus on how he made that much money to begin with? In any case, we'll take a look and see what happened."

Three days later, he walked into our yard, sweating profusely. He took out a blurry photo from his back pocket. "Do you recognize this person?"

Of course I did. I knew her better than anyone else in the world. I took out her crumpled, faded photograph from my pocket.

The detective nodded. "I figured it would be someone you knew. We checked the CCTV in the bank, and it turned out that this girl brought in your account book, seal, and power of attorney, and showed the deposit slip."

"But how could they let someone who isn't the account holder leave with all that money?" Mr. Cho cut in.

"She even knew the PIN. You told it to her?" he asked me.

I shook my head. She didn't even know I had those numbers. The warden had told me he would keep my account book and stamp safe for me, and that I shouldn't tell anyone my PIN.

The detective explained that Yong-ae had given the correct PIN and hadn't roused any suspicions. "Don't worry," he reassured. "We'll find her soon."

"No," I said.

"What?"

"You won't be able to."

The detective clucked and addressed Mr. Cho. "What is he, slow? Doesn't he understand what's happening to him?"

By the time immigration authorities sent the detective a fax in response to a document request, he had realized that I wasn't slow. In fact, I had known exactly what was happening, even predicting his failure to find Yong-ae. It turned out that Yong-ae had left the country at 6:25 p.m. on April 22 on Northwest flight 296 to Mexico City.

The detective shook his head in dismay. "She's clearly a pro. You've been tricked by a con artist."

But I didn't mind that she had taken the money. I never cared for money in the first place, and I would have used it for her anyway. So she had just taken what was rightfully hers. "She's not a con artist," I said.

The detective looked exasperated. "She's not a con artist? They took your money and fled."

"Who?"

"She left with some guy named Yun Yong-dae. He pretended to be some kind of a social worker or something, but it turns out he was a fraud, too. The defector organization was in name only. He set it up to take in all the government funding he could." The detective studied the printout again. "She's hot. She must be clever, too."

I snatched the photo out of his hand. I recognized her middle part, her long lashes, and her pert nose. She had stood erect, confidently, as if she had known someone would study her every move.

The detective wiped his shiny head. "They're in Mexico by now. You might as well just forget about getting the money back."

I could forget about the money, sure. But I wouldn't be able to forget her. "Yong-ae's gone to America," I announced.

"No, I told you, they went to Mexico," the detective said. "Well, I guess they could be on their way to America. Defectors who settled in the South aren't recognized as refugees, so the only way they can get to America is to cross illegally from Mexico or Canada. Going to Canada or Mexico is much easier with a Korean passport than to America."

I had my path laid out before me. I would go to Mexico and smuggle myself into America.

✪ ✪ ✪

Four weeks later, a letter arrived to my attention. It came in an airmail envelope rimmed with red and blue stripes. It was from a Claire Kang, but there was no return address. Over the stamp were the words: "New York."

Mr. Cho glanced over at me. "What is that?"

"Something beautiful." I ripped the envelope open. I thought I could smell her fragrance.

Dear Gil-mo,

I'm here in New York. Every morning, I eat a bagel and look out into the city from my narrow window. My window's pretty dirty and it streaks when it rains. Is it raining where you are? I go to this café where I can see the Statue of Liberty and drink coffee. I think about all the places we passed through. The industrial neighborhoods of Seoul with black smoke thick in the sky, the night stage in Macau and the lights shimmering in the harbor, the haze surrounding Shanghai, the stinking streets of Yanji, the pebbles on the bottom of the river that tickled my feet as I crossed, the prison camp with rusted steel and smoke. That's our past, whether we like it or not.

I can't say I'm sorry. I know I took everything you had, but I don't think it's helped me much. Yun Yong-dae, that prison camp butcher who toyed with our lives—I couldn't stand it when I thought about everything he did to us. I swore I would kill him if I ever saw him again. But when I landed in Seoul, he vouched for me. He told them we'd known each other since the camp, so I found myself making a happy face. Do you know how he came to be so accepted in the South? He told them he had been imprisoned! When he was the one who imprisoned everyone else! He made up a fake organization, supposedly to help defectors. He pocketed government funding, sold fake information about North Korea, and paid for his lifestyle with rewards he got for accusing defectors he didn't like of committing espionage.

You couldn't have really believed that I was this hotshot spy—or did you? I was just a pawn in his grand scheme. See, we made a deal. He would inform on me and accuse me of being a spy, then I'd be put in prison and go on trial. By the time they figured out that I was a nobody, he would have already taken the reward money. We'd go to America. He needed my looks and I needed his skills. He told me how he put you up to steal the in-

heritance from a homesick old man's family. He told me about the account and the money. He didn't know your PIN, though. I was able to figure out what it was, since I guessed it would be in our language, but I didn't let on that I knew while I was in prison.

The investigators suspected that Yun didn't have the right information about me. Or maybe they never believed it from the beginning. But the government needed a distraction like that, since the administration's approval rating is so low. It's a great story, don't you think? A femme fatale who seduced loyal soldiers into handing over secret information. Eventually, everyone moved on and I was released after signing an affidavit that I would be loyal to the South.

So then we took your money. I don't know how I could do that to you. What's wrong with me? I hope you can figure that out. I feel like you're the only person who really knows me.

Yong-ae

Finishing her letter, I sat for a long while. *What's wrong with me?* I knew it wasn't necessarily the money she had been after. She hadn't been able to elude the warden's grip. It wasn't just her; I had also relied on him, believing blindly in whatever he told me. Maybe we were too used to obeying him; after all, he protected us while directing our lives. It occurred to me that we were like ducklings bonding to whatever they saw when they first hatched, whether it was a tractor or a duck. This wasn't her fault, just like nobody could fault ducklings for trailing after a tractor.

DAY SEVEN: MEXICO

August–November 2007

From the far end of the hallway, Angela's footsteps approach, low and sturdy. The door opens and she enters, holding a thermometer. I'm sitting at the table, rubbing my thighs with my palms. She pulls a bouquet of flowers from behind her back. They're all different colors, shapes, and sizes—seven yellow freesias, seven red roses, five green canna lilies, seven lilies, and three reeds. The sweet scent of freesias envelopes me. "They're beautiful," I say. "They must have been expensive." I undo the arrangement and sort the flowers into five bundles. I hand her the freesias first. She takes them, looking puzzled, but inhales their scent. I then hand her the roses, then the cannas, then the lilies.

"You don't like them? Why are you giving them back?"

"I'm not giving them back. I'm giving them to you."

She just blinks.

"You gave me this, right?"

She nods.

"Then it's mine."

She nods again.

I hand her the reeds. "I want to give you a gift, but all I have are these flowers."

She changes the subject. "All the crimes you've been accused of until now are acts that you didn't entirely understand. Or others used you without your knowledge. But illegal entry—this is different."

"I can't tell you that I'm not an illegal immigrant," I admit. "I came into America illegally. I crossed the Sonora Desert."

"Even the fittest have a hard time crossing it. How were you able to cross? Hundreds of migrants lose their lives there every year."

"There's magic in this world. And miracles."

Angela looks frustrated. "What magic?"

"I was sent to America by the Messiah. He put me on a donkey and I crossed the desert."

"You're delusional," Angela says, sighing. "How did you even get to Mexico in the first place?"

"After Yong-ae left, Mr. Cho found me a broker, who wanted twice as much as the going rate because of the way I am. He told me to contact him when I had all the money."

"And how did you get all the money?"

"I had kept 200,000 won in cash in my room. In three months, I managed to multiply it a hundredfold by playing the stocks. Then I got on a plane to Mexico."

HOW TO CROSS THE DESERT

The local broker was waiting for me in the Mexico City airport, wearing a short-sleeved shirt printed with large flowers and green vines, holding a big placard with my name on it. He was Asian and fluent in Korean, but introduced himself as Jesus. His body language and expressions were Mexican. His white teeth shined against his darkly tanned face, and he had a round stomach. He motioned for me to follow him. I hitched my knapsack over my shoulder and stepped into the dry heat outside.

Jesus opened the back door of an old pickup in the airport parking lot, revealing two men sitting inside. One was Korean with a Seoul accent who introduced himself as Jang Ju-han. He had bankrupted his small business and was headed for a new life. Jesus later let it slip that Jang was actually going to America to escape his creditors. The other man was Kim Yong-jo, an ethnic Korean by way of Yanji. An illegal immigrant in South Korea, he figured he might as well go to America to make more money if he was going to be looked down upon by his own people in Seoul.

The pickup passed an empty lot piled with tires and a gloomy industrial area. Different smells came at us at each new intersection. Mildew, something rotting, the sting of chemicals. The truck stopped at a shabby motel on the outskirts of the city. Jesus told us to get some sleep. He would be back at five in the morning. He drove off, leaving a trail of exhaust behind him.

The next morning, he knocked on our door, right on time. We rubbed our eyes and trudged out after him. The truck sped through the darkness. At Central Station, Jesus handed out train tickets and we all settled into our seats. "This is the best way to do it," he explained. "Thousands die on the tracks going to Rio Bravo." As the train left the city, the scenery turned bleak. Rocks, sand dunes, and low brush flew by, and the train rattled precariously across a ramshackle bridge and a tall rocky gorge. The brush turned into a thicket then became sparse. The desert appeared. The train slowed to a stop in the middle of the desert. Mexican immigration officials herded illegal immigrants riding on top of the train, and we watched the desperate hide-and-seek of the hunted from the comfort of our windows. Police dogs paced outside and a helicopter hovered overhead. Thirty minutes later, the train began to move again.

We got off the train in Torreón. According to Jesus, we were moving by car from this point on, as it was easier to fly under the radar that way. Another pickup truck was waiting for us. We began to drive through the billowing dust. I fell asleep. When I woke up, the sky was a dark scarlet. We drove on for two days straight. I threw up a few times, my stomach churning from the constant bouncing and rattling. My head throbbed and my body felt liquefied. There was no longer any brush around us.

38 km to the border
Drive slowly
Welcome to Ciudad Juarez

We drove past a plaza in the center of Ciudad Juarez. Small groups of bedraggled people huddled on the church steps. We arrived in front of a run-down motel.

"We've made it this far," Jesus said, smiling broadly. "We're close. We're halfway there." He gave each of us a big hug. The others grinned as though they had already become American citizens. "We'll be staying here for about two weeks to get you ready to enter America."

We were forbidden to leave our room. Jesus stopped by once a day to give us provisions that would help us get to America. One day it was rain clothes and work gloves, and the next day it was an inner tube. Sometimes he woke us early in the morning and made us pack up and move, playing hide-and-seek with border agents.

Two weeks passed, then another. We were still in Ciudad Juarez. The other two became anxious. Our costs were increasing. They were starting to get cranky and angry, their hope and optimism wearing down.

"I'm going to end up dying here, right next to America!" Kim groused.

Jang told him to shut up. Their argument grew into fisticuffs. "I can't do this anymore!" shouted Jang. "I'd rather die on the way there. I'm going to insist that we cross, now."

The next day, Jang demanded a refund if he wasn't going to be able to cross.

Jesus looked helpless. "You think I want to be here?" he snapped. "I can't tell when the route will open. Shut up and sit tight, unless you want to get shot up by border agents. I can't wait for this to be over, too."

"What is it going to be, a month? A year? You want me to just keep trusting you?" Kim joined the argument.

Jesus put the arm of his sunglasses in his mouth. "Look. You could fill a baseball stadium with all the people I helped into America. I've done it every which way. I've swum across, I've sailed across—"

"Did you also walk on water?" mocked Kim.

Jesus ignored him. "I even went through Altar. I walked through the desert for ten days with a Honduran family of five!"

"You expect us to believe that?" Kim retorted.

"That's entirely up to you. But if you want to get there, just shut up and wait."

Kim rubbed his beard sullenly.

"Is it hard to cross the desert?" I asked.

"Are you kidding?" Jesus pushed his sunglasses on the top of his head. "Everyone thought I was crazy for trying. God doesn't open doors for those who fear, you know. You have to knock. I knocked, and, even though we almost died, the door opened."

"How?"

"You have to keep three things in mind when you cross the desert. You have to throw away your map and follow the stars. The desert geography changes every few hours because of dust storms, so maps are useless. You just follow the North Star. The second is that you have to believe that you're not alone, even when you are. As soon as you begin thinking you're alone, you lose the will to continue. Finally, you have to rest along the way, no matter what. If you don't rest, you can't keep going. These three things can help you cross any desert in the world." Jesus pulled the sunglasses down back over his eyes.

"Don't tease the kid," Kim snapped. "If you can cross that easily, we'd have become American citizens a long time ago."

Jesus glared at him and stormed out.

"Fucking piece of shit. He's full of it!"

✪ ✪ ✪

Good news didn't come, only bad. Two boys crossing the river in the middle of the night got swept away by high water. The

Americans doubled their border patrol. A seventeen-year-old Honduran boy lost all his money to a coyote. A twenty-two-year-old Nicaraguan girl was shot by a gang member. Coyotes had the ability to pluck out those with money. If someone didn't have money, they took whatever you had that might make them money. They would tell you they'd help you cross the river for 200 pesos, then take all your cash and clothes once you were on the riverbank. Competition between groups of coyotes was fierce. People were beaten and stolen from, but they couldn't complain. Police were paid off to look the other way. The desperate swam recklessly across the Rio Bravo and drowned, or they ended up staying in Mexico and living in a haze of drugs.

I counted my blessings that Jesus was looking out for us; he seemed trustworthy and catered to South and North Koreans, Chinese, and Filipinos. But the waiting dragged on and people kept getting caught. Local papers reported the list of people who were caught attempting to cross the border as if it were the daily weather forecast. We huddled over the paper and I read out loud, detailing how underground tunnels and sewers under the border were discovered by American authorities. "Look here," Kim addressed Jesus. "The U.S. Border Patrol is catching hundreds of illegal immigrants every day. They're pouring in surveillance equipment and thousands of soldiers. What are you doing to get us across?"

"You have to read between the lines," Jesus said placidly. "Sure, seventeen were caught. But that means nearly 1,200 made it. That means nine out of ten succeeded. Why else do you think Bush is sending troops and money to the border?"

Kim glared at him.

"When all the conditions are perfect, we'll cross. It'll have to be when the patrol is a bit lax, when the moon isn't so bright, when you're at your peak physical state. My partner on the other side is going to tell me when the searchlight or surveillance equipment is down, okay? And then, when you cross, it's done. You'll get in a limo my partner hired and you'll sail through the checkpoints. They never check the expensive cars. You'll unpack your things in a fancy hotel and take a hot shower. And your American dream will have come true." He laughed, and we couldn't help but laugh along.

✪ ✪ ✪

One day, Jesus barged in and took me out in his truck. Kim and Jang demanded why they weren't being taken and where we were going, but he ignored them. He told me he would show me America. "Do you know who ends up getting to America? People who believe they can. I can tell you do. I'm going to show you America. Don't worry about getting caught. We'll be quick."

We arrived at the river. I looked across at America. I was so close.

THE SONG OF STARS, SAND, AND BONES

One early morning two weeks later, Jang ran into the room, looking pale.

Kim woke and looked groggily up at him. "Where did you go? We're supposed to stay inside, remember?"

"That asshole Jesus!" Jang said, his voice hoarse. "I should have known when he shoved us into this pigpen. We haven't seen him in the past few days, so I went out to see if I could find him. That asshole left! All that shit he told us about the limo and showers, all of that was a lie!"

Jang had discovered that the border patrol along the Rio Bravo had strengthened, and the police department of Ciudad Juarez and Mexican immigration authorities were planning a joint crackdown. Jesus's colleagues had been arrested, but he had kept us in the dark, then fled.

"What's going to happen to us?" Kim asked slowly. "How are we going to get our money back?"

"The money isn't the problem," hissed Jang. "The authorities might be kicking the door in any second! We have to get out of here."

"Where to?" Kim asked, looking panicked.

"They say the police are cracking down to the east. We need to go west. Crossing the desert to Tucson will be better."

We left in a hurry, leaving behind a mess. We walked along the street. Kim took out a peso he had kept hidden in his shoe, allowing us to take a bus. We left the city and rode along the back of trucks or a donkey-pulled cart. We walked on unpaved roads westward.

Three days later, we came upon an old wooden sign.

Welcome to Altar

We were 100 kilometers from the border. Altar was teeming with migrants trying to get into America through the Sonora Desert, which abutted Arizona; this was the largest, harshest border in the world, complete with intense heat, snakes, and scorpions. The eighty-kilometer trek across the desert didn't allow access to water, shade, or roads. Half a million migrants attempted to cross here, and most of them perished or were caught and deported. Kim and Jang were paralyzed by fear; they wanted to find a coyote to identify a safer route. I told them I would cross alone.

"Gil-mo, forget what Jesus told us," Kim advised. "He was a crook."

I ignored him. I began my preparations. I would need to drink two gallons of water every eight kilometers. If I brought too much water, I would be slower and become more dehydrated, and if I had too little I would die of thirst. I bought provisions. I estimated the coordinates based on the map and decided to walk with the sun on my right shoulder. The hot white mounds were gently sloped, and the sand underfoot grabbed my ankles. Sweat evaporated before trickling down, the salt clinging to my skin. I walked toward the center of the desert; it sucked every bit of moisture from my body. My legs felt detached from the rest of me; my head burned. The length of my gait was thirty-eight centimeters; after four thousand steps I took a sip of water and ate a cookie. I was dizzy and parched; the heat was exhausting. My body ached. The sun toasted me then peeled my skin, layer by layer. I kept forging ahead, one step at a time.

At night, the roiling sand cooled. I walked on, looking up at the stars. I could hear them singing, filling the quiet desert. Father had told me people became stars when they died. I stared up at the faces of the dead. The sky spun, dunes rose and fell, and sand blew into my mouth. A lizard skittered across the sand. Stars twinkled above and bones of the perished sparkled below. I lay next to the bones and talked to them, but they replied that they were resting, sleeping, never to wake. I lay in the sand bed with the wind as my blanket.

A large city appeared. The enormous skyscrapers of the American city I saw online, the wide boulevards. Someone beckoned at me, his hair dusty, his face worried. He came to me stiffly and looked at me with lifeless eyes. I knew him. Father, you said heaven was quiet and bright. This must be it. The sun is so bright. The world is all white.

But my son, this isn't heaven. It's the desert.

Father, I met Jesus. He dipped me in the river and promised me he would take me to America.

Father's lips cracked. He disappeared into the sandstorm. Sand, wind, and the sun rushed toward me, baking me. I saw Yong-ae's face. I saw heaven. I calculated the 9999th prime number. Numbers told me where to go. They ordered me to put my foot forward, then the other foot. Soon, I couldn't take another step. The last step I took went into nothing. The sun spun once in the sky. Everything turned black.

I opened my eyes. The sun was waning. Sand flitted around, twinkling. I smelled something odd. A donkey approached me. Its eyes were gentle, and its coat glistened gold. It showed me its back. *Where do you want to go?* it asked.

Can you take me to America?

It nodded its thick, stout head and grunted. It began walking through the desert, across the vast sea of sand. Its legs weren't long but it trudged on steadily. The wind erased the footprints we left behind.

I came to. I saw a black stretch of tar ahead. Asphalt. The road heading to Tucson. A giant red Coca-Cola truck sped by with a roar, sand swirling behind it. It was November 18, 2007. I had crossed time and space to arrive in America. Jesus was right. I followed the North Star, walking along with Father and the donkey. I rested during the day to be able to walk at night. He hadn't lied. He had pulled me through the guts of the desert.

✪ ✪ ✪

Angela stares at me. "This story is different from everything else you've told me," she says slowly. "You're acknowledging that you committed a crime."

"Should I not?"

"I don't know. I think I may have wanted you to be innocent somehow."

DAY SEVEN: NEW YORK
November 2007–February 2009

I emerged from the desert and hitched a ride on a freezer truck packed with frozen sardines, then a refrigerated truck holding dead chickens, before getting in a container truck with thousands of boxes of canned tuna. Finally, I sat next to a bankrupt supermarket owner as he drove a rattling Ford sedan. I entered New York in an electrician's truck with a broken air conditioner; I noticed how nicely people were dressed, and how busy they all seemed.

I began working at an upscale Japanese restaurant called Nozomi. My cooking skills came in handy. Nozomi was popular with Hollywood glitterati and politicians. The restaurant had two entrances; the main one was decorated with Italian marble and Indonesian volcanic rock, and was frequented by Wall Street fund managers, PR firm executives, investors, politicians, and actors. They arrived in expensive cars for their reservations, made six months in advance. The other door led into the alley, which reeked of rancid oil and garbage. Kitchen staff and waiters huddled out there, smoking. Tall gray buildings lined the alley, casting it in dark shadows all day.

My colleagues in the kitchen were all ages and from all backgrounds with one thing in common—we were all poor. We had all come here searching for something better. Ricardo came from Puerto Rico with dreams of buying a small food truck. Salim, a Pakistani, yearned to obtain a green card in order to give his children a decent education. They emptied trash, washed the floor, and wiped the trays clean.

I was promoted to a cook within six months of working at Nozomi. Wearing a white chef's coat, I rinsed and made rice, fluffed it with vinegar, and trimmed raw fish. I rinsed rice, poured water on it, put it on the stove, and watched steam escape from the pot, smelling the sweet scent of rice. I scooped perfect, glistening rice into bowls. This was all I had dreamed of when I used to go hungry.

Beautiful customers laughed in the dim dining room. I watched them surreptitiously, dipping my fingertips in water and grasping a small mound of rice doused in vinegar. Exactly 328 grains. A few extra grains made it hard for the rice to spread easily in the mouth, and a few less made it less satisfying. I held a slice of fish in my left palm and smeared some wasabi on it. I put the ball of rice on top and pinched. I did this with the fewest movements; the longer it stayed in my hand, the more I touched it, the less fresh it became. Waiters glided around and people talked in hushed tones. Dishes clinked. People came in and left. At the end of the night, I went home through the alley door.

✪　✪　✪

Every Monday when Nozomi was closed, I took out my favorite black-and-white-striped shirt to go see someone. I got off at South Ferry and walked past the Starbucks and the bodega to get on the Staten Island Ferry. It smelled of gas and water. Leaning against the railing, I watched the water slapping against the side of the vessel. Plump seagulls followed us, snatching crumbs thrown by tourists. I turned to look at the Statue of Liberty—she was 225 tons, 46 meters tall. Including her pedestal, she was 47.5 meters tall. Or 93.5 meters tall if you measured from the surface of the water. Over the last 120 years, she watched as travelers, immigrants, and fugitives stepped off old steamships from Ireland, Poland, or Germany onto the putrid docks with sea legs, their eyes dreaming of freedom and plenty. I wanted to be greeted with her torch but felt undeserving.

You're an immigrant, too, she said gently. *I welcome you.*

But I'm not here legally.

Leaving someplace to go elsewhere is an issue separate from laws. Legality isn't a factor for me. An immigrant is an immigrant. You can stay here for as long as you want.

Time had dyed green her Grecian gown and crown. White clouds floated among buildings. Yong-ae was here somewhere. I knew she was. I looked for her on my way to the fish market on my bicycle, on my way home, on the train to South Ferry, among the crowds I watched on the morning news, on the stage of a small club in a back alley. I never spotted her, but I knew she was here somewhere. I knew she looked up at Lady Liberty from a café somewhere, the same Lady Liberty I was looking at now.

Do you know Yong-ae? I asked Liberty.

I'll tell you if she comes here. I've seen everyone who has come to this city.

The wind picked up. Shallow waves dotted the surface of the water. Seagulls cried overhead and the ferry followed the river. I thought back to the afternoons along the Taedong, that river teeming with gray mullet, the senior colonel waving at us from the deck of the USS *Pueblo*. I wondered about the statues of the Great Father and the Dear Leader, gleaming in sunlight— will they be pulled down one day, hanging from a big crane, their ankles chopped off and their waists severed? The engine groaned as the boat sliced through the water.

I got off the ferry and looked down into the water at the crushed plastic cups and pieces of Styrofoam floating around. I perched on a railing, my legs dangling in the water, and stared up at the Statue of Liberty; everything about her highlighted the beauty of the golden ratio. Her height, the distance between her shoulder and her hand holding the torch, the distance between her eyes and forehead, the length of her forehead and cheeks, the length of her lips and the width of her face, all of it. The water lapped my calves and toes. I fished my legs out and hugged my knees to my chest, looking into the blue-green eyes of Liberty. Her dress turned golden in the sunset. As night fell, the city lights glimmered on the river. I stuck out my hand to feel the water. I just had to figure out where Yong-ae was.

THE REASON WE NEED TO BE HAPPY

I returned to the apartment I shared with Ricardo after saying goodbye to the kitchen staff. We had been laid off last night. I picked up today's *Wall Street Journal*.

Last Sunday, the American financial system was thrown into turmoil. Following the demise of Bear Stearns in March, Bank of America took over Merrill Lynch on Sunday and Lehman Brothers was shuttered after 158 years. The Federal Reserve and large investment banks are searching for emergency solutions for the economy. Citigroup, Credit Suisse, Deutsche Bank, and a dozen other investment banks were given $70 billion.

Jonathan Fox, head manager of ICP Capital, said, "Monday will be the market's final judgment. The warning bells are ringing, and people are fleeing." The crisis is compounded by the fact that Lehman Brothers and Merrill Lynch were the two pillars that supported Wall Street over the last century. Analysts are expecting the housing market to plummet.

Antonio Hardy, a ninth-year employee at Lehman, said he was planning to clean out his desk Monday morning. "We worked hard here. Now everything's gone. I can't believe it."

I folded the paper and began to pack.

"What are you going to do?" Ricardo asked, looking stunned and weary.

"I'm going to go to a secondhand car dealership in Queens."

"They're hiring?"

"No, I'm going to make myself a job."

We wandered among the dust-covered cars and settled on a small yellow truck, a roach coach with a stove. We pooled all of our savings. Ricardo liked the cheery yellow, and I was partial to the Coca-Cola logo painted on the side. It had sat in the lot for two months; it was covered in dust and the inside was caked in grease. Ricardo bought rubber gloves, washed the truck, and converted the workstation into a sushi bar.

Two days later, we prepared sushi the same way we had done at Nozomi. Ricardo drove around, picking out the freshest fish in the markets at dawn. I made perfect rice. Around noon, people poured out of buildings; they had at least survived the morning. Though layoffs were followed by more layoffs, people still had to eat.

Ricardo bantered with customers in front of the truck. "For the price of a McDonald's hamburger and a Coke, try sushi made personally by Matsumoto Yoji, who was Nozomi's star chef!"

Fund managers, investment bankers, accountants, and lawyers queued up. I made sushi after sushi. It became quiet again after 1:30. Nothing was left; neither rice nor fish. Ricardo grabbed a fistful of crumpled bills and grinned. "Matsumoto, if we keep going like this, we're gonna be rich!"

"You be rich. I have to find Yong-ae."

"How about you find her after you get rich?"

"Finding her comes first," I told him. "After that I'll worry about getting rich."

✪ ✪ ✪

Nights passed and mornings went by foggily. Yong-ae was nowhere to be found. Had she merely been a figment of my imagination? I looked out at the streets from inside the sushi truck, always searching for her. I looked for her in the early morning markets, on the Brooklyn Bridge, in the water below. I had painted her portrait on the side of the truck. I put her in a hat with a purple flower in it and a fur cape. Customers often asked who she was.

"That's Yong-ae," I told them. "We're connected."

Nobody was interested in the mathematical principle behind our connection. "Okay, if I ever see her I'll tell her you're looking for her," they told me.

People smiled when they ate my sushi. I could see their shoulders relaxing.

✪ ✪ ✪

Two days later, as I made my 353rd sushi that day, happiness walked toward me. Her ankles were still pale, but she now had sunken cheeks and rumpled hair. Bedraggled pigeons fluttered up. She walked straight up to the truck, staring at the singer who had once mesmerized Macau painted on the side. She raised her sunglasses onto her head. "I've been watching from across the street," she said. "I recognized you instantly." The blue around her eye wasn't eye shadow. She smiled, wincing.

I stared at her. What had happened to her?

Ricardo silently cleaned up and folded down the awning. He started the truck. Yong-ae and I sat side-by-side in the passenger seat. Streets passed quietly and slowly, muted. Ricardo let us out by the river. We could see the Statue of Liberty shrouded in vapor.

"So here we are, in the land of the free," Yong-ae said bitterly. She pushed her damp salty hair away from her face, wincing.

"Who did that to you?"

"You don't need to know," she said tersely.

"He's terrible."

"How would you know?"

"He only gave you a bruise on one eye." If she had another bruise, at least she would return to her beautiful symmetry.

Her long hair tickled my cheek. "Odessa became destitute," she said suddenly. "His business collapsed. He left Wall Street, fleeing fraud charges. He escaped overseas." She hesitated, then showed me her left hand. A gold ring. "It's a wedding band."

Was it time to congratulate her? Who did she marry? I had so many questions.

"I married Yun Yong-dae," she spat out, finally. "I mean, Steve Yoon. He changed his name."

I must have looked puzzled.

"I was undocumented, just like you. I needed to become legal. So I begged him to marry me. He's become an American citizen."

"How?"

"He knew he couldn't apply for refugee status, since he had become a South Korean citizen. So he told them what he knew about the prison system and drug operations, some true, some not. It worked."

I stared at her.

"He wanted us to get in with Odessa so he could help us climb the ladder, so to speak. I was supposed to get to know Odessa, introduce him as my uncle, help him get him a job at his company, so he could act like a real investor. But then the financial crisis hit."

"So what is he doing now?"

"He spent all the money we brought from Seoul. All your money, that is." She glanced at me. "I also took money from Odessa's company. But it's all gone. He stays in our old rental place in Queens, drunk. Whatever I bring home he drinks up, then beats me, telling me to bring home more."

I shook my head. "Why are you staying with him?"

"I have to stay with him until I get my citizenship." She sounded forlorn.

✪ ✪ ✪

Yong-ae came to visit me at the truck every day after lunch rush. Bruises moved from eye to cheek to lips to neck. "He thinks I'm seeing someone else," she explained.

"It's true, isn't it?"

"I don't want him to know. He's going to try to use you again." Her voice hardened.

I couldn't just watch her suffer. "Why don't I come over one night?"

She hesitated.

"If I'm there, he won't beat you," I reasoned.

"Do you think so?"

"He knows I can make him money," I said. "Why would he do something I'd disapprove of?"

A few days later, I arrived at the decaying neighborhood they lived in. The buildings were run-down, and damp walls had dead, dry vines tangled on them. Their house was surrounded by a nice grove of cedars, though. The warden opened the peeling front door, assuming a cheerful expression. He looked older and worn. "Great to see you, Gil-mo!"

He led the way into the house. The crossbeams were exposed in their living room, and the furniture was old.

Yong-ae came out of the kitchen, drying her hands. She opened her mouth to greet me.

The warden cut her off. "What a great occasion this is! Let's celebrate. We're all together again."

The kitchen table was draped in a white tablecloth and set with nice dishes. The warden heaved himself onto a chair. "Eat up, Gil-mo!" He served me some spicy chicken.

I took a bite, but I felt hungry and sad. Yong-ae brought some rice to the table.

"You'll make us a lot of money, won't you?" The warden grinned.

Yong-ae's face crumpled. "Leave him alone," she hissed.

The warden lifted her chin with a finger. Her thin gold necklace glinted in the light. "Oh, come on. I'm his guardian, remember? I have his best interests at heart." He smiled kindly at me and served me some bok choy.

We all relaxed eventually. The warden topped my glass with more Coke. "Let's try one more time," he said suggestively. "This time we can make a ton of money in America."

Yong-ae frowned.

The warden kept downing glass after glass of whiskey, his face growing redder and his voice booming louder. It became late. By now, he was completely drunk. He ruffled my hair and hugged me jovially, laughing. He reeked. I shoved him away.

"Hey! I watched over you after your father died. I made sure you got your resettlement funds when you got to Seoul. I taught you about capitalism!" He had suddenly turned into the warden I had known, with his red insignia and a hand on his leather belt. He grabbed me by the throat and dragged me into the living room. My stomach somersaulted.

Yong-ae rushed after us, pulling on his sleeve. "Stop! Don't hurt him!"

He flung her aside with shocking force. He opened the bureau in the living room and pulled a handgun out. "Back home I used to get rid of dozens like you," he slurred. "I received the Medal of Honor for that."

Yong-ae lunged at him, and he smashed the gun into her temple. She slammed into the ground, blood trickling down her face. He shoved me against the bureau. He pulled her up by the throat and forced her to kneel; he placed the muzzle of the gun to her temple, giggling.

I caught my breath. I grabbed a golf club leaning against a cabinet. I lifted it over my head but he whirled around; the club missed and struck the hand holding the gun. A shot rang out. Fire shot up my right thigh. The warden dropped the gun, cradling his wrist. I moved toward the gun, but my leg dissolved and I fell. I managed to wrap my hand around the gun.

The warden's face darkened. "Gil-mo," he said gently. "That's dangerous. Put it down."

The warden had sent countless people to their deaths. He had taken all the money I had. He ruined Yong-ae's life, and now he was trying to kill her. I knew what I had to do to fix it.

Yong-ae grabbed me around the waist. "Stop, Gil-mo! Put it down!"

I stood, trying to shake her off. I leaned on the wall. The ground was slippery. She refused to let go, but I pushed her off. She spun in place, hit her head against the wall, and fell. The warden rushed at me.

Another bang. My entire body was vibrating. Nothing else hurt. The warden fell to the floor. Something red splashed the walls.

I had kept my promise to Mr. Kang. The warden's death smelled metallic. I limped to the table, yanked off the tablecloth, and wiped the blood from the wall and floor. I took a bottle of antiseptic from my knapsack, folded a napkin into eighths and wiped the greed and hypocrisy from his face. I closed my eyes and prayed. His death would be delivered to hell, I hoped.

A dog barked from far away. Sirens wailed and cops were shouting. Blood kept trickling down my leg. I sank into darkness.

✪ ✪ ✪

Angela covers her face. She rubs her eyes with the tips of her fingers and sighs. "So, did you kill Steve Yoon?"

"No."

"Then who did?" She sounds relieved.

"The bullet."

Angela lets out a sigh and clasps her hands together. "I don't know what to think here."

"It doesn't matter if you don't believe me."

She shakes her head. "I may have wanted you to lie, at least this time." She reaches over to touch my hand but stops, remembering that I don't like to be touched. She closes her eyes for a moment, then opens them and gets up.

"You don't need to take my temperature or a blood sample?" I ask.

"No, not today. You're well now. Maybe you were always well." She leaves the room, holding my file against her chest.

INTERROGATION OF AHN GIL-MO, SUSPECT IN THE MURDER OF STEVE YOON

On February 28, 2009, at 12:30 a.m., suspect Ahn Gil-mo was arrested in a house in Queens, New York, under suspicion of murdering Steve Yoon, the CEO of Friends of Freedom, a North Korean human rights organization. Suspect was held in the infirmary due to a bullet wound to the thigh. He refused to speak. It was determined that the suspect had Asperger's syndrome. Over seven days, interrogation was held in tandem with psychological counseling.

1   Re: Counterfeiting of four passports

The suspect is a refugee who escaped North Korea and crossed into China. He appears to have possessed passports of various nationalities to escape the instability of DPRK. He did not use a counterfeit passport to enter the United States.

2 Re: Suspicion of possessing stolen property

When residing in Pyongyang, the suspect received a notebook from Senior Colonel Park In-ho, the superintendent of
the USS *Pueblo*, but the charge of theft or robbery was not
established.

3 Re: Charge of being an active member of Fierce Dragon Society, the largest gang in northeastern China

After escaping to China, the suspect was employed in a
syndicated bar in Yanji. The owner was the head of the gang.

4 Re: Activity as drug mule

The suspect delivered one bag to Shanghai, but it appears
he conducted business without comprehending the conse-
quences or knowing the contents of the bag.

5 Re: Overseeing and laundering funds for Kunlun Corp., a drug
gang in Shanghai

The suspect worked as an accountant in Kunlun Corp.
under the name Jiang Jiajie but wasn't directly involved in
raising or overseeing funds. He did not understand the pur-
pose of the funds. He was imprisoned for his participation in
the gang and served his sentence. No cause for a charge.

6 Re: Organizing a fraudulent gambling ring in Macau's
Tomorrow Casino

While working as a janitor in a casino in Macau, he studied
the roulette games and the house edge and won $59,000. It
appears that this was earned through mathematical calculations, without the use of violence or fraud.

7 Re: Participation in a gun battle between illegal gambling organizations on the Macau shoreline road that left eleven dead in
February 2006

The suspect was involved in a physical altercation between
illegal gambling organizations. At the time he did not possess
a weapon and left the scene.

8   Re: Inheritance fraud committed in Seoul, South Korea

The suspect was involved in a fraud organized by Yun Yong-dae (Steve Yoon), who defected from North Korea. Yun, who was active as an unofficial correspondent and contact for separated families, disguised the suspect as a relative of a wealthy man and stole a large inheritance. However, the suspect did not understand the plot and the inheritance was clearly given of the deceased's own accord. He was cleared of suspicion by South Korean authorities.

9   Re: Complicity with a North Korean spy active in Seoul

The suspect has known Kang Yong-ae, who was arrested in Seoul under suspicion of spying, from their time at a prison camp in North Korea. During trial, Kang was cleared of suspicion.

10   Re: Manipulation of stock prices

While residing in Seoul, the suspect made large profits through internet stock trading, but these were the results of thorough market analysis. The suspect's volume did not amount to artificial manipulation of the market.

11   Re: Illegal entry into the United States

In 2007 the suspect entered the United States illegally through the Sonora Desert and moved to New York. He is charged with illegal entry to the United States.

12   Re: Murder charge on February 28, 2009

The victim Steven Yoon threatened the suspect's life in prison camp and stole his assets in Seoul before fleeing to the United States. As the victim threatened Kang with a gun, the suspect believed his life to be threatened and fired the victim's gun during a fight in self-defense. Given that the suspect did not flee the scene, it does not appear to be calculated and premeditated.

Of the twelve grave crimes the suspect is charged with,

the majority are not merited as they do not meet the requirement for intent or because the suspect acted in self-defense. After treatment over seven days, the suspect showed that he could not separate reality from fantasy. His mental state revealed that he believed his distorted memories were reality. Appropriate psychiatric treatment is needed. Deportation to South Korea is recommended.

—Angela Stowe, Special Agent, Counterintelligence Division, FBI

I AM A LIAR

After I leave the infirmary, I am held at a shelter for deportees. As the bullet missed bone, my injury heals quickly. I won't have a limp, which would ruin the symmetry of my gait. Over two months, the investigation continues to resolve my refugee status and criminal charges. After numerous psychological inquiries and interrogations, Angela's report is accepted. Yong-ae and I receive deportation orders.

I pack my belongings. I put my triangles, my old calculator, and my ruler into my knapsack, along with several pairs of underwear and clothes. I'm reminded of the day I left the prison camp. I flip through Captain Miecher's notebook. I never did end up getting this notebook back to him. I slide it into the inner pocket of my jacket.

Yong-ae and I have checked in at the airport when we notice Angela. She came to say goodbye. We have about ten minutes before we have to go. We go to a small café. Yong-ae helps me take my knapsack off and put it in my lap. Angela brings over two coffees and a Coke. "I wanted to apologize," she begins.

"Why?"

"I didn't tell you the truth. I'm not a nurse, I'm an FBI agent."

I look out the window at the runway. Airplanes glide down and float up, and move in slow motion toward the terminals.

"I was brought in because the sequences and symbols at the scene weren't easily decipherable. I majored in math, and I've cracked codes. That's why I pretended to be a nurse. To try to engage you with math. I'm sorry. I used the love you have for numbers to trick you."

"That's okay," I say. "I knew you were fooling me from the very beginning." I look off into the distance.

"You knew? You didn't say anything!" She's quiet for a moment. "Fine. It doesn't matter. I do have a final question, though. You wrote, 'I am a liar' next to the body. The first sequence revealed your talent for math and the second told me you like prime numbers and symmetry. Were you riffing off the liar's paradox with the sentence?"

The phrase *I am a liar* is meaningless, but a paradox emerges in the process of proving its veracity. If the sentence were true, then the speaker would be a liar. But since he would then be telling the truth, the speaker couldn't be a liar. On the other hand, if the sentence were false it would mean the speaker was not a liar, but the sentence itself would then be a lie. The sentence always produces a contradictory result. "It's also an illustration of Gödel's incompleteness theorem," I tell her.

Gödel had proved the liar's paradox through numbers. His first incompleteness theorem posited that as long as a calculation-based system was not contradictory, there was always one problem that could be neither contradicted nor proven. His second incompleteness theorem stated that if a system satisfying the conditions of the first incompleteness theorem claims it is consistent, one couldn't prove or disprove that.

"So you're saying that you wrote that to trick the investigators. To trick me." Angela looks pained.

I nod quietly.

She smiles bitterly. "If it's true that you're a liar, then you're a liar. Your story is a lie. But since we figured that you were truly saying you were a liar, it means you're not a liar. If the sentence is supposed to be a lie, then you're not a liar. So that's how you get away with it."

"Not everything was a lie," I correct. "I wanted to tell the truth. I told lies only to show the truth."

"So what was a lie?"

"I can't explain all that. I guess I'd say that they were all truths. All for one lie."

"You mean when you said you killed Steve Yoon."

I nod.

"Why did you lie?"

A thin line appears between Yong-ac's brows.

"It wasn't Yong-ae, either," I explain. "She was just tussling with him, her hand on his hand holding the gun."

Angela's eyebrows twitched. "So you thought she would have to rot in prison her entire life. And that's why you decided to say you did it. What a sacrifice!"

"It wasn't a sacrifice."

"So what's the truth?"

I look up at the ceiling and sip my Coke. "There are things that are true but can't be proven, remember?"

She lets out a long sigh.

I pull out the notebook from my pocket and hand it to her. "This is Knight Miecher's notebook. I've had this for the last ten years. You should have it. I won't be back in America, and if he's alive he's probably in the United States somewhere. If you take it there's a higher chance that he'll get it back."

She flips through the dog-eared notebook. An announcement blares on the PA system. I put my knapsack over my shoulder and get up. Angela gets up, too. She reaches over but stops herself. I give her a hug. She smells warm. I finally let go and Yong-ae and I walk to the gates. I don't look back.

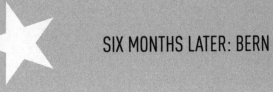

SIX MONTHS LATER: BERN

THE WINNER TAKES IT ALL

It's early morning in September. The mist over the Aare River drifts over the streetcar tracks as buses trundle along wet streets and bicycles glide by. On Spitalgasse, men and women in suits hurry along. The clock tower bell chimes, and bears and acrobats pop out and begin dancing. We pull into the square and head east as the bell rings for the tenth time. Credit Suisse provided us with a luxury car because of Yong-ae's VIP status, with $8 million on deposit. Two weeks ago, we made an appointment to withdraw everything and close the account. The car stops in front of the main branch. A guard runs down the stone steps to greet us as our driver gets out of the car and fixes his black cap. The guard opens the back door. I push my sunglasses up my nose and get out. Yong-ae follows suit, smiling at the driver. We follow the guard up the stairs, through the heavy revolving doors, and into the quiet lobby topped with tall ceilings and crystal chandeliers. Paintings surround us—are they Klimt? We cross the large marble hall, Yong-ae's heels tapping out a cheery beat.

The teller greets us behind the gleaming oak window. Yong-ae fixes her makeup and slides her small mirror back in her Hermès crocodile bag.

The teller slides across a sheet of paper. "Please write down your PIN and we'll be able to assist you with your transaction."

Yong-ae glances at me. I write down: 9643052178. The magic spell Mr. Kang talked about, one that reveals the numbers you don't know, just like a dictionary. It has to be the one that unlocks the bank account in Yong-ae's name. She trembles in anticipation. I tap a finger on my thigh. Time ticks by slowly.

The teller taps on his keyboard and hits enter. Eight million dollars shoots through cables into Yong-ae's Citibank account. "Here's your receipt."

Yong-ae takes off her gloves and counts the zeros. Exactly six. "Thank you." She puts her gloves back on.

We cross the lobby. Yong-ae's shoes sound more confident than when we entered. The guard opens the large glass doors and we step outside. Yong-ae slides into the back seat. She takes her sunglasses off. "To Central Square, please."

The car takes off over cobblestone streets. The radio is playing ABBA's "The Winner Takes It All." ABBA, that perfect symmetry.

The gods may throw the dice / their minds as cold as ice. / And someone way down here / loses someone dear. / The winner takes it all. / The loser has to fall . . .

Who is the winner? Me? Yong-ae? Both of us? Who was the loser? Yun Yong-dae? Fate? Did we really take it all? Outside, hard stone pillars and marble buildings pass by. Yong-ae hums along. We turn a corner. We spot the red awning of an outdoor café. Yong-ae asks the driver to let us out in front of the café.

We sit side by side under the sun. Her black dress fits her perfectly. Her eyes are bruise-free. Her bangs are in perfect symmetry. She orders an espresso. I order one, too, and also hot water and an empty cup. I pour the espresso into the empty cup and use the espresso cup to pour in three and one-sixth cups of hot water. The ratio of 1:3.14 between coffee and water is the most harmonious. We take in the sunlight, people strolling by, the scent of the breeze. A long time later, she gets up and checks her makeup with her small mirror again.

"I'm going to go to the bank and make sure the money came through." She finishes the rest of her espresso and walks away without looking back. Her shadow glimmers for a long time after she turns the corner. I sip my cooling coffee.

Thirty minutes pass. One hour. She isn't back yet. The sun is setting and the dome on the other side of the street glistens in bronze. She's still not back. The wind turns chilly. People hurry home. The waiter comes around several times in exasperation. I take out a notepad and a pen.

Dear Yong-ae,

The waiter asked me how long I was planning to stay. I told him I was waiting for you to come back. He suggested it would be better for me to wait for you at home instead of sitting here alone. Nobody's ever alone, are they? The clock tower in the square ticks every second, people are walking by, the street cleaning car comes by, the dolls pop out of the clock tower at the top of every hour to dance, and people are playing chess on the board drawn in the street. I'm not alone, see?

The waiter suggested that you weren't coming back, then shook his head and left. Maybe he's right. Maybe you won't come back. After all, you have a lot of money in your name. You used to leave without warning, without hesitation. But I know you'll come back in the end. So I'll just wait here for you.

Remember Captain Knight Miecher? I called Angela a few days ago to see if she was able to find him. There was no such name on official lists for the USS Pueblo, POWs who returned home, or those who died in battle. As she cross-referenced names, she came across a man who had been on the USS Pueblo, Graham Johnson. His wife's name was Elizabeth—the "abeth" referred to in his notebook. Angela tracked down her address in Atlanta, and visited to give her the notebook. She found out that Captain Johnson had died three years ago. And since the senior colonel didn't know English, the greeting, "Nice to meet you!" sounded to him like a name. See, the world isn't too big, and everyone knows each other somehow.

It's getting dark in the square. Stores are turning on their lights, making old metal signs shine. It started raining, and it smells like dirt. It has been 12,814 seconds since you left—3 hours, 33 minutes, and 26 seconds.

Yong-ae is standing in front of me. "Sorry. I know you've been waiting forever."

I put down my pen and kiss her on the cheek. She puts an arm around my shoulder, looking abashed. "I had too much to do. I decided to go get my hair done and then go shopping. I bought these diamond earrings and this ruby necklace at Tiffany's, and then got these heels, and stopped by to get my nails done."

"You don't need all that to look nice," I tell her.

"Shall we go?" Yong-ae asks.

"Where?"

"Let's go to the nicest hotel in this town." She steps down onto the wet pavement and waves her hand.

A black taxi slides up like a large, gentle animal. She beckons to me. I run over and get in the car with her.

"Bellevue Palace Hotel, please," she says.

We have nowhere to go, but tonight we will stay in this city.

AUTHOR'S NOTE

Many people helped me, both directly and indirectly, in writing this book. My deepest respect goes to the defectors from the North, whose strong passion for life and dedication to seeking freedom prevailed despite their many hardships.

During the writing process, I consulted various records authored by defectors who settled in South Korea, as well as hundreds of writings and memoirs posted online by the defector community. These sources helped make my story more detailed. *Total Control Zone* by Ahn Myong Chol, *The Aquariums of Pyongyang* by Kang Chol-hwan, and *The Hidden Gulag* by David Hawk informed my understanding of the conditions in the political prison camps. Choi Jin-yi's *The Woman Who Crossed the Border Three Times* inspired the storyline about underground Christianity in the North.

I consulted various books about math and science, including Kasuga Masahito's *How Was the Poincare Conjecture, A 100-Year Unsolved Question, Solved* and I. Bernard Cohen's *The Triumph of Numbers: How Counting Shaped Modern Life*. Douglas Hofstadter's *Gödel, Escher, Bach: An Eternal Golden Braid* was immensely helpful in building the overall structure of the novel, and Bruce Schechter's *My Brain Is Open: The Mathematical Journeys of Paul Erdös* gave inspiration for Gil-mo's trajectory.

Gil-mo's experiences in the United States are indebted to the following: Steve Donahue's *Shifting Sands: A Guidebook for Crossing the Deserts of Change* gave important inspiration for imagining Gil-mo's crossing into the United States; reporter Ahn Yun Seok's personal blog, *Ahn Yun Seok's Pyongyang Report*, and reporter Song Gyong-hwa's *Hankyore* series about defectors' American dreams helped me envision the life of North Korean refugees in the United States. I also referred to various photographs of areas and people within North Korea, interviews with North Korean citizens and defectors, and documentaries about defection. I am grateful to countless people who are too numerous to mention here.